Palo Alto City Library

The individual borrower is responsible for all library material borrowed on his or her card.

Charges as determined by the CITY OF PALO ALTO will be assessed for each overdue item.

Damaged or non-returned property will be billed to the individual borrower by the CITY OF PALO ALTO.

P.O. Box 10250, Palo Alto, CA 94303

GAYLORD

BURIED CAESARS

BURIED CAESARS

CAESARS

STUART M. KAMINSKY

THE MYSTERIOUS PRESS

New York • London • Tokyo

CT

 The Mysterious Press, 129 West 56th Street, New York, N.Y. 10019

Printed in the United States of America.

First Printing: April 1989

10 9 8 7 6 5 4 3 2 1

Library of Congress Cataloging-in-Publication Data

Kaminsky, Stuart M.
  Buried caesars : a Toby Peters mystery / by Stuart M. Kaminsky.
    p.   192
  I. Title.
PS3561.A43B87   1989
813′.54—dc19   88-25449
ISBN 0-89296-374-3   CIP

To Natasha Melisa Perll Kaminsky

The President of the United States ordered me to break through the Japanese lines . . . for the purpose, as I understand it, of organizing the American offensive against Japan, a primary object of which is the relief of the Philippines. I came through and I shall return.

General Douglas MacArthur
Friday, March 20, 1942,
in Adelaide, Australia

1

There was no point in trying to talk to Major Castle.

We were sitting in the back of a big, 1940 custom-built Packard Darrin Victoria One-Twenty watching the coast go by and the sun go down. The driver was a tall, dry bolt of a man whose name I didn't know but found out later. Castle hadn't given it to me when he picked me up in front of my office on Hoover Street in Los Angeles.

Castle hadn't told me much on the phone when he had called. He said he was on a mission for General Douglas A. MacArthur. The mission involved me. He asked if I would meet him but the request sounded more like an order. It was the kind of request I might consider turning down if I had a few bucks in the bank and he hadn't suggested that the outcome of World War II was about to be laid on my battered desk.

It was September 1942, a clear Tuesday during which I had done some shopping—three pairs of socks and a new shirt from Hy's for Him on Melrose. That left me with enough for a bag of tacos from Manny's and gas to get my bleached Crosley through the next week.

Major Castle had come when I clearly needed a client.

I had shaved in the morning, gone shopping and waited to change into a pair of new socks and the fresh shirt until I got to the office I shared with Sheldon Minck, D.D.S. Sheldon was off that day on a mission of his own, the nature of which he did not share with me.

I had suggested to Castle that I meet him in front of the Farraday Building. The alternative would have been for him to pass through the dark pit of tooth decay that was Shelly's dental office, past the spit sink, into the Cabinet of Dr. Caligari I used for an office. It wasn't impressive enough for army brass.

Just before four, when I was scheduled to meet Castle, I had checked my face in Shelly's mirror. Flat nose, graying hair, lopsided smile. The body was a slightly bulky 165 pounds on my five-nine frame, but that didn't hurt when your business was looking like a mug and occasionally acting like one. A half century of abuse had molded my body for the job. The bad back didn't show and the scars were covered by clothing.

I thought I was ready for Castle. The Packard was waiting in front of the building, windows closed in spite of the eighty-three degree heat. The driver was standing next to the car, not leaning on it, his hands at his sides, his crisp tan suit and tie in contrast to my almost matching baggy trousers and jacket. My tie was loose. I'd gotten a deal from Hy on the shirt but the collar was a half size too small.

"Mr. Peters?" the driver asked softly over the rumble of traffic and the laughter of a woman shopper and her dour companion, who blitzkrieged past me on the sidewalk.

"Peters," I agreed.

The driver nodded toward the Packard and got in the driver's seat. I opened the front door and a voice from the back said, "Back seat."

I closed the front door, opened the back one, and slid in next to a man who looked as if he had been dipped in cement the day before. The man was gaunt and gray. His hair, cut close, his face, his hands, his eyes and even his suit were gray. He turned those gray eyes on me and I didn't like what I saw in them. Shelly's office wouldn't have bothered Major Castle. He had seen far worse.

"Major Oren Castle," he said, holding out his right hand as the car pulled into traffic.

I took his hand. In spite of the heat in the closed car, the hand was dry and cool.

"Toby Peters," I said. "Where we going?"

"Not far," he said.

"You mind telling me what this is about?" I asked.

"Yes," he said and looked forward.

That was all anyone said in the car for the next hour and a half as we drove over to Daly Street and headed north. Every few minutes

I'd take a look at Castle to see if I could catch him blinking. I never did.

I watched the landscape which was fine but I'd seen hills before. Boredom set in after three minutes and then I wanted the flash of the city, the noise of a downtown L.A. street or restaurant, the blare of a movie. Nature and I got along okay, but we weren't exactly pals.

We hit the valley and turned east south of Glendale, where my brother Phil and I had grown up. The sun was half red and half reflection on the horizon behind us. The driver turned right when we hit Hill Avenue in Pasadena. After ten or twelve minutes of twists and turns we pulled into an iron-gated driveway just beyond the Huntington estate, and drove along between thick trees which blocked the view of the house until we were almost in front of it. The main house was a big adobe with barred windows and turrets. It was supposed to look like old money and old Mexico. It looked like someone with a lot of money trying for the effect and coming pretty damned close.

The driver parked in front of the front entrance and he and Major Castle got out without a word. I got out and closed the door. I didn't say anything either. The driver was standing at the top of three red stone steps, right hand clasping his left wrist as he looked down at me. Castle stood next to him looking at me over his shoulder, waiting. I moved toward the steps and Castle went to the door and knocked.

I joined him just as one of the thick wooden doors opened on a well-groomed woman in a tan dress. Her dark hair, swept up in the latest style, framed her long neck; her jeweled earrings caught the last light of the day. She backed up with a small smile and we stepped in.

Inside I could see that the woman was older than she had appeared at first glance; older but still worth looking at.

"He's waiting," she said.

Castle nodded and moved past her.

"Good to meet you," I said to the woman as Castle's shoes clicked on the inlaid tiles.

She smiled. Nice mouth. Good teeth. Clear skin.

We moved, Castle leading the way. The walls were draped with colorful rugs and the rooms were tastefully furnished with solid, old-looking wooden furniture. Castle stopped in front of an inlaid oak door and knocked. He looked directly at me and I thought I detected something in his face that might pass for life.

"Come in," came a deep voice and in we went, Castle letting me step past him.

It was an office, a big overheated office; desk, bookcases, photos on the walls, plenty of big-leaved plants. Next to the desk, his hand on the back of a leather chair, stood General Douglas MacArthur. Even in civilian clothes there was no mistaking him. His face was on buttons, posters, front pages, ads. There had been days named in his honor, parks dedicated to him. He was the only hope California had of keeping the Japs from landing tomorrow afternoon. He was, as one citizen had said, the greatest general the United States had known since Sergeant York.

The General examined me and then turned his eyes toward Castle, who stepped out of the room and closed the door. I knew MacArthur was sixty-one or sixty-two, but he looked younger. His shoulders were broad and he looked a little thin. He was slightly stooped. His hand went to his thin dark hair, which he had combed back to unsuccessfully cover a bald spot. He was dressed in a white suit with broad pleated pants and he stood still for about ten or fifteen seconds as if he were posing for a portrait. I'd already begun to sweat in the small, hot room, but MacArthur looked cool and clean, without a stain.

"Mr. Peters," he said. "Sit."

It was a command. I sat in a heavy wooden chair in the center of the room in front of the desk. MacArthur examined me, puckered his lips, nodded in what might have been acceptance and reached for a cigar which was smoldering in an ashtray on the desk. He took a puff, played with his finely manicured fingers and began to slowly pace the room. MacArthur was giving me a minute to get used to being in his presence. As he got absorbed in what he was saying, he began to pace more quickly.

"General Douglas MacArthur is not here," he said, starting to pace.

"I can see that," I said.

He either ignored me or didn't hear. The General went on pacing.

"It is vital that no one know I am here," he said. "Communiqués are being issued in my name from my headquarters in Australia. I am in radio contact by the hour. Within three, possibly four days I will return to the Pacific, but it is imperative that my presence in the United States not be revealed."

"You're not here," I said.

"I'm not concerned, Mr. Peters, about the possibility of your revealing my presence to the press," the General said, shaking his head and pointing his cigar in my direction. "You do not have sufficient stature to make such a revelation credible."

"Thanks," I said.

"My people would simply deny it," he said. "And I assure you that I will not be in this house for more than three hours. The Japanese would give a great deal to know my whereabouts, and I doubt that my passage back to Australia would be without incident if they were to find out. It was only through perseverance and good fortune that my family and I managed to get through the Japanese blockade of Corregidor earlier this year."

"I know," I said. "General, whatever you want . . ."

"Please do not interrupt," he said with a tone that made it clear he was not accustomed to interruption. "Your very obscurity is an asset in the situation, that and your reliability. My people tell me that you are tenacious and loyal. Both attributes I value. Your intellectual capacity and lack of flexibility may not qualify you for a field commission, but given the present circumstances . . . your full attention is required here, Mr. Peters."

My eyes had wandered for an instant to a photograph on the wall showing a younger MacArthur and a cowboy with a big nose and white hat. The cowboy, Tom Mix, had his arm around MacArthur's shoulder and both were grinning at the camera. "I'm sorry, General," I said.

MacArthur had followed my eyes and moved to the photograph, cigar in hand, to straighten it in case my gaze had moved it off center.

"I'm partial to Western movies," he said. "Always have been. I'd see one every day if time permitted. The codes are simple and clear.

Good and evil are immediately discernible and honor is the highest attainment."

"In the movies," I said, readjusting my sweat-moistened underwear and turning so I wouldn't be tempted to look at the photographs instead of the General, who obviously had his own show to put on for a two-bit private detective.

"This war will last no more than two, possibly three more years," he said, pacing again. "Those who predict fewer have not taken heed of the determination of the Japanese and the terrain in which the troops of General Douglas MacArthur must do battle."

He paused to look vaguely in my direction. I nodded wisely. A knock at the door and the good-looking woman with the earrings came in with a pitcher of iced tea and two glasses. She put the tray on the corner of the desk and tiptoed out as if she were in a cathedral.

MacArthur poured two tall glassfuls and handed one to me. An ice cube crackled in my glass. I was afraid it would upset the General, who had taken a quick sip and was pacing, pausing, smoking and talking once again.

"When this war is over," he said, "and the rising sun has set, this country will have to turn its attention to the next threat to the people of not only the United States, but the entire free world. Do you know what that threat is, Mr. Peters?"

I considered several possibilities—dehydrated coffee, near beer, French and German opera—but I kept my mouth shut, confident that the General had the answer or he wouldn't have asked the question.

"Communism," he said softly, almost resignedly; then his voice rose in determination. "If it weren't for the Axis, we would be fighting Communists in the plains of Asia and the vineyards of Europe. I am not a fanatic, Mr. Peters. I am a pragmatist. This country will require a leader who is not afraid to face a further conflict, a leader whose hands are not bound"—and with this he held out his hands as if they were cuffed together—"by an executive branch more interested in its political perpetuation than in the need to make difficult and unpopular decisions to safeguard the shores of our country. And who will that leader be?"

I had a feeling I knew the answer to this one.

"Someone," he continued, "who has the trust of the people and the vision to deal with broad global issues. The irony here is that less than a year ago, General Douglas MacArthur was retired and on the way to being forgotten. Now . . ."

MacArthur walked to the window behind the desk and motioned for me to come. I got out of the chair, feeling a slight twinge low in my back from the long ride, the moist underwear, and the rigid chair. I gulped down my tea, plunked the glass on the tray and moved next to the General at the window, wiping my brow with a less-than-clean handkerchief I found deep in my pocket.

"What do you see out there, Mr. Peters?" he asked.

I was beginning to understand the game. He would ask me questions and I would keep my mouth shut. What I saw was a lawn, a big green lawn lined with tropical trees. Across the lawn, the tip of the sun barely touched the distant hazy horizon.

"You see," he said, not disappointing me, "the lush, trim solitude of the Pacific Coast. This tranquillity stretches along the coastline of California and north into Washington and Oregon. Our President and our European allies would prefer to ignore this vital Edenic garden of America, but the Jap is not ignoring it. A Japanese submarine has shelled the coast of Oregon at Fort Stevens. Japanese airplanes have dropped incendiary bombs on southern Oregon. At my urging, antiaircraft batteries and barrage balloons are going up around defense plants in California."

He paused to watch the effect of all this on me. I tried to look affected.

"General Douglas MacArthur," he went on, "commands the troops of nations with inadequate supplies diverted to an assumed victory in Europe. My ships, my men, battle vigorously. Today we turn back the Japanese at Guadalcanal and hold our own in New Guinea. The tide has begun to turn. The Battle of Midway will prove to be the pivot, and the world will have to recognize what I have accomplished and with how little. General Douglas MacArthur will have protected the coast, won the war. Of that I have no doubt."

I grunted and looked at MacArthur, whose hands were folded

behind his back. He looked at the lawn and trees for a few minutes with a small smile, and ended with a sigh.

"Funds have been quietly raised to mount a political campaign in my name at a point in the future when such a campaign will be appropriate," he said, resuming his pacing. "A civilian aide of mine, Andrew Lansing, has stolen these funds."

"How much did he take?" I asked, moving to pour myself another glass of iced tea. The speech was over. We were getting down to business now. I didn't know anything about war and armies, but I'd spent a lifetime with thieves.

"One hundred and eighty thousand dollars in cash," MacArthur said. "But he took something much more valuable: a pouch of documents outlining my political campaign and a list of donors to that campaign. Present donors and those who have pledged support in the future."

"You want me to find Lansing and get the money and the papers back," I said.

"Precisely," MacArthur said. His eyes were probing now. He was trying to decide something. I had the feeling he had more to say but wasn't quite sure it was safe to say it to me. So I went on.

"Why not have some of your own people to do it? The army. The F.B.I. The cops."

"And risk the information getting out that I am actively pursuing the office of President of the United States? Roosevelt would have an excuse for removing me from command in the Pacific, and I tell you, Mr. Peters, without Douglas MacArthur, who has the respect of the people of the Pacific Islands and knowledge of that theater, this war might be prolonged for years."

"What aren't you telling me, General?" I asked.

MacArthur's face went tight and taut. A flash of anger opened his eyes and passed and when the anger passed MacArthur took a deep breath.

"You have no children?"

"No," I said.

"I have a son," he said. "I want my son to be proud of his father, his country. Arthur is the complete center of my thoughts and affection. I feel I am very fortunate in having him and my wife, Jean, in the twilight period of my life. Do you follow me, Peters?"

"Right into battle," I said. "But something's still missing."

"All right," MacArthur said with a deep sigh. "About five months before I was named Chief of Staff in 1930 I met a young woman in Luzon. I was divorced from my first wife, Louise, and . . . I met Isobel Rosario Cooper, the daughter of an Oriental woman and a Scottish businessman living in the Philippines. Isobel came to Washington and with my support lived in a suite in the Hotel Chastleton. I was, at the time, living with my mother in the Chief of Staff's quarters in Fort Myer. My mother, and the press, were less than tolerant of such liaisons. My mother, whom I loved dearly, was most protective of my honor and my career. When I was a cadet at West Point, she took rooms nearby so she could actually see my window."

"That must have been reassuring," I said.

"I do not tolerate mockery, Mr. Peters," MacArthur said, stopping suddenly and glaring at me. I apologized. MacArthur went on pacing and talking.

"I provided Isobel with all of her needs, money, an enormous wardrobe, even a poodle. Even the staunchest of us are the potential prey of our animalistic tendencies."

"I know," I said, and he nodded, acknowledging my support.

"Isobel began to deceive me, see other men, comment on our relationship in public," he said. "I had to end the relationship. A short time later Isobel sold my letters to her to Drew Pearson, the columnist. I paid Pearson a substantial sum to suppress those letters. Supposedly, this money was passed on to Isobel. I had done nothing illegal, but it was vital that my mother not know."

"Lansing has the letters," I said.

"Precisely," MacArthur answered. "The letters, campaign information, money. It is not only my honor and political career which are in jeopardy. My very image as husband and father might well be tarnished in history, beyond repair."

I should have asked MacArthur why he kept the letters, but I could see the strain in his eyes. The General was not accustomed to confessions. Maybe it was a little easier because I was a stranger, a detective, and someone he had reason to believe was discreet.

The General paused, pulled himself together, and stood at attention, his back straight, his shoulders squared. I felt like saluting but I didn't know how. He moved toward me and put out his right hand. I took it and felt his grip tighten. I had the fleeting feeling that I had just witnessed one hell of a performance.

"Major Castle will serve as liaison on this operation. He will answer your questions, provide background, make arrangements, supply you with whatever support you might need. I will see you as needed or not at all until you've accomplished your mission. Do you have any questions?"

I had a lot of them but I also had the feeling that the General didn't want to hear them. He moved in front of me as I got up and put his hand on my sleeve.

"I can't overestimate the importance of this mission, not only to me, but to the future of this nation," he said confidentially.

I was convinced. The future of the human race was in my hands. The General took my arm, looked me in the eyes and smiled sadly at having put such a burden on one so unworthy. But his benevolent smile also let me know that he had faith in my ability to get the job done.

He guided me to the door and opened it. I stepped out.

"We will meet again, and soon," he said and closed the door, leaving me alone with Major Castle who stood at ease a few feet away, waiting, his eyes on me.

"Follow me," Castle said, and I followed him back the way we had come, into a living room decorated in early conquistador. He pointed and I sat in a bright chair with a Mexican rug on it, and reached over to touch an ugly clay statue with buggy eyes, no body and a limp penis. Castle disappeared in the direction of the office, where I assumed MacArthur was watching the last of the setting sun. He returned a few minutes later and handed me a leather pouch.

"Everything you need is in there," he said.

"Money," I said.

"Three hundred dollars. If more is needed . . ."

"More isn't needed," I said.

"There's a complete biography of Andrew Lansing, including relatives, friends, acquaintances, organizations to which he belongs. There is also a detailed statement indicating the events that surrounded the act. The General would like you to read the material and then ask me any questions you might have. I'll have sandwiches and beer brought in for you while you read."

"I'd like to take this back to L.A.," I said, holding up the hefty package, "and read it tonight, without you looking over my shoulder."

"That won't be possible," said Castle. "Two days have already passed since the money and papers were taken. Another day could . . ."

I got up and handed the packet back to Castle.

"Forget it," I said. "I'd like to save the universe, or at least lower California. I really would, but it'll have to be my way. I've had the feeling since I got into that spiffy Packard with you and Tonto that I was being treated like a little boy who's supposed to be quiet in front of the adults and do what he's told. Well, Major, it doesn't work that way. Not for me. I'm not in your army and I couldn't take the orders when I was a cop or when I was working security for Warner Brothers. I didn't warm to the uniforms and I didn't enjoy feeling like if I went down there'd be another like me to pick up the flag."

If I'd expected to get Castle angry I'd failed, but I hadn't really expected it. I had read those eyes right. I needed room and respect. I couldn't buy it with my clothes or my bank account. It was time to take a stand.

"At the battle of Missionary Ridge, in the War Between the States, General MacArthur's father did just that," Castle said. Our faces were inches apart. "He picked up the flag of the 24th Wisconsin and led a charge that broke the enemy and turned the battle. He was eighteen. They gave him the Medal of Honor."

"It sounds dumb to me," I said.

"You have something better to do with your life?" Castle asked.

"Maybe not," I said. "It depends on how you look at things."

"Honor," said Castle. "Loyalty. They're the only things worth living for."

"How about a taco, a good night's sleep, and a dark woman?" I said, our noses almost touching.

Castle broke first. My guess was that he didn't want to go back to MacArthur and let him know I was causing trouble.

"You win, Peters," he said. "We do it your way. Corporal Chester will drive you back to Los Angeles. I'll be in touch with you at ten hundred hours tomorrow."

I considered a few more questions, but Castle turned and left the room.

I went out of the house and got into the Packard. This time I got in the front seat. The sun was down and Corporal Chester was relaxed. He was a different man away from Major Castle.

"A tough man," I said.

"The General or the Major?" Chester said, his eyes on the road.

"Both."

"Been through a lot, said Chester. "Major was on Bataan. Escaped. Made his way to Manila. Hid in a wine barrel for a week while the Japs looked for him. He was nuts, the way I hear it. Filipinos helped get him to some island. Way I hear it, the Major—he was a Captain then—didn't talk, didn't sleep. They got him to Australia and MacArthur took him in, took care of him, gave him a field promotion. That was only a few months back."

"So Major Castle may not be back from Bataan yet," I said.

"He may not be back from the dead yet," said Chester. "But he's a good soldier and he'd die for the old man."

"And you?"

Chester shrugged.

"I'll do what I have to do. My brother died somewhere in the Solomons last month. General had you in the hot room?"

He glanced at my limp hair and soaked shirt.

"Man's immune to heat," I said.

"Man changes his clothes six times a day," said Corporal Chester. "Probably changed just before you got there and stepped into the room from outside. Eisenhower was the General's adjutant for years. One of my buddies heard Ike say he'd studied acting under MacArthur for three years."

We didn't say much more the rest of the trip back. I suggested that we stop for a beer, but Chester didn't have the time. He had to get back to San Marino before midnight.

Just before nine-thirty he dropped me in front of the Farraday.

"I'll see you," I said. "Thanks for the ride."

Chester didn't say anything but he did nod as he drove off. Twenty minutes later I parked my Crosley in front of Mrs. Plaut's boarding house on Heliotrope in Hollywood.

2

Down the street and inside one of the small box houses that had gone up during the first boom of the war, a woman was crying; farther away, traffic in the direction of Wilshire echoed an occasional outlawed beep from an impatient driver. I knew I had no hope of getting up the porch steps, into the house, and up to my room before Mrs. Plaut caught me. I had never made it before and nothing had happened to make me think tonight would be different. I was right. Mrs. Plaut was sitting on the porch in her wicker chair, a neat stack of papers in her lap, staring down at me as I tucked the pouch Major Castle had given me under my arm and moved resolutely forward.

"I am morose," Mrs. Plaut announced.

She was a small but not frail broomstick of a woman with a cotton billow of white hair. At the moment she was wearing a gray dress and an orange sweater. No one knew her age, probably not even Mrs. Plaut, but boarders' estimates ranged from seventy-eight to three hundred. The three hundred guess was from Joe Hill, the mailman and oldest tenant in the boarding house.

"I'm sorry to hear that," I said, moving across the porch, knowing I would never make it to the door.

"Would you like to know why I am morose?" she asked, without turning her head to me as my hand touched the doorknob.

There was no help for it. I turned, leaned against the white wooden wall, clutched the pouch to my chest and said, "I certainly would."

The woman down the street let out a wail of anguish. My guess was a late-night battle with her husband or boyfriend. In this neighborhood, it usually was.

"It is not that I don't have things to be thankful for," she said. She paused, but I had given her all the encouragement I had the heart for. "I shall tell you a few of the things for which I am thankful and then I will inform you of why I am morose," she went on.

"Mrs. Plaut." I tried holding up the pouch. "I have a lot of work to do. I've got a job. I'm supposed to save General MacArthur's reputation and possibly the United States or at least California."

"General Douglas MacArthur has no need of your services, Mr. Peelers," she said with a sigh. "You are joshing me again. The MacArthurs are self-sufficient. We, the mister and I, briefly lived two doors from the MacArthurs in Milwaukee. The older general, Douglas's father, Arthur, was a stately man."

"Things you are grateful for," I reminded her.

The woman down the street had settled into a soft sobbing and the faraway traffic sounds had faded. There were crickets chirping in the warm darkness and I felt sleepy.

"I am grateful that my hearing device is no longer on the fritz," she said, pointing to the hearing aid I had bought her. "I am grateful that Evelyn Ankers and Richard Denning have just been married. I am grateful that I have my health, a breathing canary, all my teeth, a subscription to *Liberty Magazine*, and that my book is almost completed."

"You have much to be grateful for," I agreed, fearing what was coming next.

"And now you will discover why I am morose," she said, nodding her head. "There are three reasons. First, I have discovered that the photograph which you gave me and which has hung on the wall of this very porch for some months in spite of being shot by one of your friends was not, as you had told me, Marie Dressler, but Eleanor Roosevelt."

"I never told you it was Marie Dressler," I protested feebly. What I really wanted was to get undressed, shave, have a bowl of cereal and get some sleep. I could wait an hour or so for my nightmare.

"I respect Mrs. FDR," said Mrs. Plaut, "but as you know I am not of the Democratic persuasion."

I considered asking her if she were a Tory or a Whig but I managed to hold my tongue.

"Therefore," she went on, "I have removed the photograph and, since the fault was yours, I believe you should replace the photograph with one of Marie Dressler or someone of comparable ilk."

"I'll do my best," I said. "Now I really . . ."

"Two," she continued, ignoring my whining, "you have not read or edited my manuscript for some time. I am not a young woman. I do not have all day."

Mrs. Plaut had for years been writing the history of her family. It had reached mega-epic size, several thousand pages, each neatly printed with random tales of confusion and family myth. I had discovered the plot of several familiar movies and novels in her pages, including *Wild Boys of the Road*. I had read the pages because Mrs. Plaut was convinced that I was an editor and exterminator, not necessarily in that order.

"I'm sorry, Mrs. Plaut," I said, reaching for the manuscript pages on her lap.

She handed them to me.

"Pay particular attention to the disclosure concerning Aunt Eloise and the three-footed duck," she said.

"Three-footed duck," I repeated. "Got it."

"It was not a real three-footed duck," she said confidentially, urged on by the crickets in the front lawn. "It was a fraud perpetrated by a Mr. Victor Sensibaugh of Seattle for the purpose of bilking money from widow women."

"I look forward to reading it," I replied. "Now I've really got to . . ."

"I said that I was morose about three things," she said, holding up three fingers now that her hands were free of manuscript. "The third thing is that the Farmer's Market at Third and Fairfax is having a sale on beef tongue, twenty-nine cents a pound."

"Why does that make you morose, Mrs. Plaut?"

"Because I am unable to take advantage of this once-in-a-lifetime sale," she explained. "Mr. Wherthman is usually a tiny gentleman and drives me to such sales, but he is, as you know, in Des Moines at the present."

Actually, Gunther Wherthman, who had the room next to mine in Mrs. Plaut's boarding house, was in San Francisco. Gunther, who stood all of three feet tall, was Swiss. He earned his living by translating most of the known languages of Europe and western Asia. The war had brought him deskloads of work, much of it for the government. He was in San Francisco translating an opera into English for the San Francisco Opera Company.

"I'll drive you to Des Moines early in the morning," I said.

"Good, and in response I'll make my great-grandmother's beef tongue pie," she said ignoring my wit.

"My taste buds tingle in tart delight," I said. "Now if I can . . ."

"I'm sorry, Mr. Peelers," she interrupted, standing up, "but I really cannot talk to you any longer tonight. I'll make up my shopping list and be ready in the A.M."

"Nine," I said.

"Eight," she countered and went through the door and into the house.

I stood on the porch for a few seconds, Mrs. Plaut's manuscript in one hand, the information on General MacArthur's case in the other. The woman down the street was no longer sobbing. The crickets were still chirping and I thought I could smell the trees.

The rest of what remained of the night was uneventful. I took a bath in spite of the trickle of water that seemed to evaporate before it hit the porcelain. I shaved as I reclined in the tub, and tried to remember the words to "Elmer's Tune." Back in my room I ignored the pouch and Mrs. Plaut's manuscript while I sat in my boxer shorts eating a bowl of Puffed Rice with too much sugar and the last of a small bottle of cream, listening to the Blue Network news.

The Nazis were pounding away at Stalingrad. Roosevelt was threatening wage controls. Wendell Willkie, for whom I'd voted, was in Turkey announcing that Rommel was losing the Sahara war.

I wished I had some fruit to slice up into the second bowl of cereal. My wants are few. I had money now from MacArthur. I could afford some canned pineapple.

The Beech-Nut Gum clock on my wall told me it was nearly midnight when I turned off the light, pulled the mattress from the bed in my single room, got on my knees and rolled over clutching one of my two pillows. My back had threatened retaliation once or twice during the day and I wanted to be sure to let it know that I cared.

I was tired but I couldn't sleep. I tried not thinking that I was fifty years old, living alone in a boarding house, and irritated that a Swiss midget was going to be out of town for two weeks. Before I could give the name *loneliness* to what I was feeling I rolled over, got up, put on the light and opened the pouch Major Castle had given me. I had trouble reading. I remembered that my ex-wife Ann, recently widowed by her second husband, was back in town after a month of recuperating with her sister in Boston. Howard's death hadn't been clean and he hadn't left her much. I decided to call her the next day.

An hour later I put the papers back inside the pouch and opened my window. I fell asleep clutching my pillow with the crickets keeping me company.

Mrs. Plaut and the dawn burst into my room around six the next morning. She stood over me in her white dress and gloves with an ancient beaded purse over her arm. Our trip to the Farmer's Market was uneventful if you exclude the battles with shoppers and Mrs. Plaut's threat to a less-than-enthusiastic butcher that "Mr. Peelers will turn your establishment in for health violations if you don't stop smoking in the store." I did manage to pick up some groceries, including three boxes of cereal and a few cans of fruit. By the time Mrs. Plaut stepped out of my Crosley in front of the boarding house, just after nine in the morning, I was in need of a quiet day, searching for a thief.

"I know how much you like beef tongue pie, Mr. Peelers," she said, standing on the sidewalk where she had followed me out of the house after we had put her groceries and mine away. "And I will have a large room-temperature slice ready upon your return."

"Thank you, Mrs. Plaut," I said, unwilling to even consider where she got the idea that I salivated in anticipation of digging into small pieces of the marinated tongue of a cow.

"And I'll also make some Colorado Mervin cookies," she mused. "Now, if you just find a suitable photograph of Marie Dressler and work on the pages of my book, you will be firmly within my good graces."

"I dream of that moment," I said.

I left her standing there and pulled away. The sun was shining. The morning was bright and promising. I had a full wallet and a job to do. If it weren't for the fact that the world was being blown apart, it would have been a great day.

In spite of the canned fruit on my shelf, the money in my pocket, and a job of work to do, I felt depressed when I parked in the alley behind the Farraday. Zanzibar Al, a derelict who lived from doorway to doorway, usually strolled my way when I parked the car and held out his hand. I usually placed a coin in his hand, in return for which he kept others of the alley from heisting the tires and breaking the windows. Zanzibar Al looked like a tuberculosis victim, which he claimed he was not. His pants were held up with a rope and his flannel shirt—he had two of them, one red and one blue—was always neatly tucked in. Zanzibar had the brains but not the inclination to get a job. He had once been a lawyer, or claimed to have been. He sounded like one when he was sober.

Zanzibar wasn't around this morning. No one was around, not even delivery men and late-arriving Farraday tenants. Everyone seemed to have taken a long Labor Day weekend in spite of the President's urging to keep working. I locked the Crosley, hoping that no one would step on it or put it in their pocket and walk off. The pouch and Mrs. Plaut's chapter were under my arm, and I carried a paper bag of stuff I'd picked up at Roscoe Wheat's All-Night Eats in my hand.

Jeremy Butler wasn't in the hall of the Farraday when I went through the rear door and pushed open the double doors near the rear stairwell. Jeremy was my landlord, a massive, bald, former pro wrestler who dabbled in poetry and had recently been wed to the equally massive Alice Pallice, former pornographic printer, now reformed protector of her husband's *oeuvre*. Great word, *oeuvre*. Gunther had taught it to me. I pulled it out privately at moments like this and said to myself, "I may look like a pug but, baby, I can pull out a word like *oeuvre* with the best of them."

It didn't make me feel any better. The hallways usually smelled of Lysol. Jeremy waged a valiant war against the grime of the Farraday and its denizens. A good part of his and Alice's day was spent scrubbing and rousting bums like Zanzibar Al. Today the Farraday didn't smell like Lysol and there were signs that filth was establishing a small beachhead of candy bar wrappers and empty beer bottles in the dark corners. A private Guadalcanal just off Tenth Street.

I bypassed the elevator and walked up the six flights. I only took the elevator when I had an extra ten minutes and a lot I wanted to think about. I didn't want to think about anything this morning. All I wanted to do was call Ann.

Shelly hadn't changed the sign on our door overnight. The sign had been through changes and variations, but it was now back to what it had been when I moved in more than five years earlier.

DOCTOR SHELDON MINCK, DENTIST, D.D.S., S.D.
PAINLESS DENTISTRY PRACTICE SINCE 1916
TOBY PETERS, INVESTIGATOR

He had learned his lesson. There were no new creative initials after his name. I'd made him remove the M.D. minutes after he had it painted on in gold.

"It means Master of Dentistry," he had whined. "I've got a certificate somewhere. I paid eleven bucks for it. Guaranteed."

The lights were on in the dental office beyond our small reception room but Shelly wasn't there. I was disappointed. God help me, I was so desperate that I wanted to see Sheldon Minck. God heard my silent prayer. When I opened the door to my office, Shelly stood reading something he had obviously taken from the open middle drawer of my desk.

Shelly's improvisation was pathetic. Shelly is rotund, bald except for a thatch of graying hair, short, seldom without a cigar in his mouth, and almost always in need of a clean white dental smock. He looked at me through his thick glasses, mouth open, cigar in one hand, and then looked down at the sheet of paper in his hand as if he were surprised to see it there.

"Don't tell me," I said, putting the bag on the table and kicking the door shut behind me. "Someone dragged you in here, forced you at gunpoint to go through my drawers and then, just as I was coming in, went through the window and down a rope ladder."

Shelly bit his lower lip, actually considering the possibility of clinging to my story or some variation on it. He eyed the bag, smelled the coffee and decided to go for something near the truth.

"I thought something happened to you," he said, putting the paper back in the drawer. "I was looking for clues."

"You know my phone number at the boarding house," I reminded him, moving behind my desk as he moved the other way. My office is not spacious. There is enough room for my desk and chair and two other chairs, one in the corner and one in front of the desk. That's it. On one wall hangs my California private investigator's license and a photograph of me and my brother when we were kids. My father, the Glendale grocer, stands between us, an arm around each, grinning painfully at the camera, probably holding Phil to keep him from ripping off my ear. Squatting next to me is our German Shepherd, Kaiser Wilhelm, who was renamed Murphy in 1916—which also happened to be the year Sheldon Minck began to practice dentistry on an unprepared public. To the left of the door was a square less dirty than the rest of the wall where a print of a smiling girl had once hung. I had put it up because it reminded me of someone. I had taken it down for the same reason. I was not in a good mood.

"Got coffee in there?" Shelly asked, pushing his glasses back up his nose and pointing at the paper bag.

I ignored his question, folded my hands and fixed him with my best Lionel Barrymore dyspeptic frown.

"Come on, Toby," he bleated. "I didn't stop for breakfast. I had to get here for a patient."

I didn't believe him. If the world were crying in pain from a massive abscess, Sheldon Minck would stop for breakfast. And Sheldon was having some fine breakfasts since being thrown out of his house by his wife, Mildred. Mildred had run off briefly with an actor who pretended to be Peter Lorre. The ersatz Peter Lorre took her for a bundle before he got shot, not by Mildred. Naturally, Mildred's response upon returning home was to kick her husband out.

Now Sheldon Minck resided temporarily in the Ravenswood Hotel on Rossmore in Hollywood. He had wanted to move into Mrs. Plaut's vacant room till he "worked things out with Millie," but I'd threatened him with certain death if he dared to move into Plautland. A man needs some refuge.

"Help yourself, Shel," I said, nodding at the bag on the desk as I sat in my chair and pushed the drawer closed. Sheldon gave me a nervous twitch of a grin, put his cold cigar on the edge of my desk and plunged his hand into the bag, coming out with a paper cup of lukewarm coffee, a limp cheese Danish and an egg and tomato sandwich on white. He sat across from me and I pointed at the bag, which he pushed toward me with his left hand as he held the Danish in his right.

"Dinner on me tonight," Shelly said, reaching his now-free left hand for the coffee. "Ahern's on Wilshire has a T-bone dinner for eighty-five cents. Soup, two vegetables, ice cream, coffee and potatoes. And the Carthay Circle has *Mrs. Miniver.*"

"I'm busy tonight, Shel," I said, after I put down Mrs. Plaut's manuscript and opened the pouch on the desk in front of me. "I thought you were busy wooing Mildred."

"Mildred's on vacation in Canada," Shelly said around bites of his sandwich. He had already flushed down the Danish.

"Vacation from what?" I asked.

"You know," he said, pointing his cup around the room. "Everything. Our separation. Everything."

"Shel, I'd like to chat, but I've got to get to work on this." I pointed at the papers on my desk.

"Can I help?" he asked, jutting out his jaw and trying to read the top sheet in front of me upside down. "Things are kind of slow today."

"You want to read the latest episodes in Mrs. Plaut's memoirs?" I asked, pushing the sheaf of rubber-band bound papers toward him.

"That would help me. Just read them and summarize. It will give me some room to save the world and earn a few bucks."

He took the pages with a shrug.

"What kind of sandwich is still in there?" he asked, playing with the bag.

"Tuna on wheat toast," I said. "I'm on a health kick."

"You gonna eat it?" Shelly asked.

"No, I was planning to plant it and start a Victory garden. Take it, Shel, and . . ."

The door to our outer office opened and Shelly reached for the bag. I beat him to it and retrieved a raspberry sweet roll. Then I pushed the bag toward him. He grabbed it and hurried out the door with his cache of sandwich and manuscript to greet what we both hoped was a patient.

I couldn't tell much about the patient with the door closed, other than that it was a man. I could hear the scrape of Shelly's X-ray machine, the sound of voices, and then Shelly's grating imitation of Nelson Eddy singing "Shortnin' Bread."

The biography of Andrew Lansing in the packet was brief, uninspiring and, at first glance, not very helpful. He had been born in Oak Park, Illinois, in 1912. Had an older sister. His father sold real estate. Lansing got a bachelor's degree in engineering from the University of Illinois, moved to California, where he worked in a contracting office in San Jose for a few years, and then moved to Los Angeles where he got involved in Republican politics. He was unmarried. A photograph of Lansing showed a round-faced, sober man with a baby face. He looked as if he were about to cry. His hair was combed back but a wisp had been allowed to drop down onto his forehead. There was a bit of pouting Bonaparte in the face of Andrew Lansing.

Most of the papers were lists. There was a one-page list of all of Lansing's nine addresses since birth, ending with one in Pacific Palisades, a house which he shared with someone named Melvin Grady Hower. Another included the names and addresses of each of Lansing's employers since he left college, and the names and addresses of Lansing's living relatives—most of whom were in Illinois—and the names and addresses of possible Lansing friends.

The last was a very short list. Major Castle had done one hell of a job, almost too good a job. I had too many names, too many leads.

The report on the actual theft was as concise as the biography and lists. A small group of individuals, unnamed, were working at the Beverly Hills home of one of the individuals, planning the eventual campaign of a certain high-ranking military officer. When the meeting ended everyone went home except, of course, the gentleman who lived in the house. It wasn't till the next morning that he discovered the documents had been taken from his safe—a safe to which he, Lansing, and no one else held the combination. The gentleman involved immediately called a member of the military who had been at the house the night before. The military man, with some volunteers, went to Lansing's house. Lansing had cleared out. There was no sign of his roommate Hower. The high-ranking military officer had been contacted. He issued orders and indicated that he would find a way to come to California.

No names, dates. MacArthur's name wasn't mentioned once in any of the material I had been given. They had closed the door a little late to keep the wombat inside, but at least they had closed it.

I had paused to look out the window and finish the last of my tepid coffee when the phone rang. Precisely ten hundred hours.

"Peters," I said.

"Major Castle," he said. "Report."

"I've read the material," I said.

"Go on," he urged.

"I had a coffee and a raspberry sweet roll," I added

"Did you have any ideas?" he asked.

"One or two," I said.

In the background, Shelly had switched to "Amapola" in his Caruso croak.

"And your plan of attack?" Castle said.

"I'm preparing grids and counterchecks," I said, looking down through my only window at Zanzibar Al, who stood next to my car. I got up and he waved at me. He pointed to my Crosley and I nodded and held up a finger. He nodded back to let me know that we had a deal. "I'm cross-indexing names, addresses, contacts, and will have agents checking possible intersections. Other agents will methodically make contact with each person on the list, starting with the most likely but missing none. All will be supplied with copies of Lansing's photograph and informed that if he is located they should get back to me immediately. I have a safe phone number they can call and I can check every hour on the hour, day and night."

"Sounds good," Castle said.

"Thanks," I said, and thought if he was buying all that crap I had a couple of Leland Stanford memorial gold spikes to sell him cheap.

"I'll check back with you at seventeen hundred hours," he said.

"One of my assistants will be here if I am out," I said.

He hung up and so did I.

My supply of Toby Peters low-cost special agents was limited, especially if I wanted to make a few bucks on this deal. My pool included a fat myopic dentist, a retired wrestler, a midget who was temporarily out of town, and maybe Zanzibar Al, who was permanently out to lunch.

If I wanted to pay a few bucks I could get Jack Ellis, who normally made his living as a hotel dick but had some free time since his disability. A trio of sailors on leave had thrown him down an elevator shaft. Jack had been hearing opera arias at odd times since then. There were a few down-and-out investigators in my league who I could get cheap but I'd have to tell them too much. MacArthur didn't want anyone to know he was in the States.

That left me, my Crosley, my .38, my bad back and my determination. I had no doubt that I could find Lansing. That wasn't the problem. The question was, could I find him before he spent all the money or turned what he knew over to someone who might use it to ruin MacArthur's political future? I had only one method. Start in the most obvious place, ask questions and follow leads, the good ones, the bad ones, the silly ones, the impossible ones. Follow leads till you found what you were looking for or till your client said "enough."

Lansing's most recent Los Angeles address was the one in Pacific Palisades he shared with Melvin Grady Hower. Castle had already been there and probably had someone checking the place from time to time, but Major Castle wasn't as devious as I was. I finished my sweet roll, swept the crumbs into my drawer, stuck my Dick Tracy badge into my pocket and considered taking my .38. I decided against it.

When I stepped into the dental office, Shelly was singing "Mimi" in a blubbery Maurice Chevalier accent, his lower lip jutting out. The patient in Shelly's chair watched him with faint amusement. There was something familiar about the thin man with the not too-clean white cloth around his neck. He seemed to be about my age. His white hair was cut short and combed straight back and up. His mustache was darker than his hair but showing signs of gray. He looked like a gaunt but elegant scarecrow. I had at least twenty pounds on him though he looked like he might have an inch or two on me. His brown eyes turned on me and seemed to see something I wasn't aware of.

"Open, open, open," Shelly said, and the gaunt man dutifully opened his mouth, his eyes never leaving mine. Shelly leaned over him, a particularly lethal, narrow and sharp steel instrument in his hand. I should have left but I wanted to place that face.

Whatever Shelly did, it must have hurt, but the man in the chair didn't move.

"Just a second now," Shelly said, his face now blocking that of the thin man in the chair. "Here we . . . go. Got it."

Shelly turned to me triumphantly, his glasses slipping down his moist nose, the bloody instrument in his hand. The man in the chair closed his mouth.

"That will do it for today, Sam," Shelly said to the patient. "I'll check the X-rays and we'll work on those teeth. Quite a challenge."

Shelly plunked the bloody instrument in the crowded sink, found his cigar in the ashtray and put it to his lips. A job well done.

The man in the chair removed the now-bloody white cloth from around his neck and got up. He wore a tweed suit and dark tie, confirming that he was much too elegant for the Farraday.

"One week," the man said in a soft, determined voice.

"One week and your mouth will look like Gable's. You have the guarantee of Dr. Sheldon Minck," Shelly said, leaning back on the sink, cigar in his mouth.

"Day after tomorrow at seven in the morning," the man said, glancing at me.

"At nine, Sam," Shelly said with a wave.

The man moved past me through the reception room and out the door. When it closed, Shelly beamed.

"See those duds, Toby? The man has money. Right off the street. Rush job. Mouth's a mess. Alcohol, drinking. Do you know what he wants?"

"Pain," I ventured.

"No," sighed Shelly. "He wants me to put his mouth in shape so he can join the army. At his age."

"What's his name, Shel?" I said.

"Sam."

"Sam what?"

"Sam. I don't know. I'll have him fill out a card when he comes back. He gave me fifty bucks cash in advance. Who needs names? But you want names, I'll get you names. You know where I put those cards?"

He moved to a file cabinet covered by a mess of old magazines, bills, letters that had never been answered, and searched the top of each drawer in the hope that a blank patient card would magically appear.

"Didn't bat an eye when I told him what it would cost," Shelly gloated. "Not an eye. Come to think of it, he didn't bat an eye when I worked on him, and he didn't want gas. Said he had some lung problems. Can't take gas. Man's a class act, Toby. Take my word for it. A banker or something."

"Lucky he found you," I said, moving to the door.

"Lucky," Shelly agreed, finding an ancient dental journal that looked promising. "Want to know where I went yesterday?" he went on, moving to the dental chair.

"Not particularly," I said, opening the door to the reception room.

"Suit yourself," Shelly said with a grin I didn't like. "Suit your very own self."

I didn't like his I've-got-a-secret smirk, but I didn't have time to deal with it. I left the office and went into the empty corridor.

Somewhere, probably in Madame Sylverstre's School of Music on the fourth floor, a man was singing scales in a desperate but elusive search for eight consecutive notes. I moved down the stairs slowly, no plan in mind other than to get to Pacific Palisades and do what I had to do.

Hoover Street was crowded with late-morning shoppers, soldiers, sailors and marines in uniform, and young women shoppers carrying packages. The non–package-carrying women would hit the streets just before dark and they would be selling, not shopping.

I turned the corner at Tenth, went halfway up the block and turned into the alleyway. This wasn't the most direct route to my car. It would have been easier to go out the back door of the Farraday the way I had entered, but I'd heard the slight creak of linoleum when I hit the third-floor landing. By the time I had reached the Farraday lobby I was fairly sure I was being followed. When I turned the corner on Tenth I was certain. I stopped in the alley and waited.

It was Shelly's patient, Sam.

We stood face to face. I wasn't sure I could take him. The man was rail-thin and sunken-cheeked, but there was something in his face that made me think this was a man who didn't know how to give up. He was certainly a man who didn't back away.

The pad-pad of laceless shoes came behind me as I stood waiting, ready.

"Is he after your limo, Peters?" Zanzibar asked behind me. "If he's after your limo, I'll crown him. We got a deal."

"We got a deal, Al," I said. "He's not after my car."

"Then what's he after?" Zanzibar Al asked, reasonably.

It was a good question. I let it stand. The traffic moved by us a few feet away, ignoring the drama in the alley.

"What's he after?" Zanzibar Al repeated. "Geez damn. The world is one hell of a flash sometimes. You know what I mean?"

"I know what you mean," Sam said, a small smile on his thin lips. "I simply want to talk to Mr. Peters for a minute or two."

"You could have knocked on my door," I said.

"Old habit," Sam said. "I used to be in the business. Pinkerton. I guess I'm not as good a shadow man as I used to be. That, or you're damn good."

"Let's say I'm damn good. It'll make us both feel better," I said.

"I feel better," Zanzibar Al said to himself behind me.

I couldn't figure Sam. My first thought was that MacArthur or Castle had sent him to keep an eye on me, but he could have done that without going through a session with Shelly. Besides, I had the feeling that I had seen him . . .

"Hammett," I said.

"Hammett," he agreed.

"I've seen your picture in the *Times*," I said.

"I had a black mask as a kid," Zanzibar Al said. "I forget the precise reason for it."

"Not for some time," Hammett said. "May I suggest we go somewhere less awkward?"

"I'll give you a ride," I said. "My limo is parked back here under the watchful eye of Zanzibar Al."

I stepped back to reveal Al, whose right cheek twitched in embarrassment.

"Pleased to meet you," Al said.

"And I you," said Hammett.

I dipped into my pocket, came up with two quarters and dropped them in Al's waiting hand. It was more than double what I usually gave him, but the fee was being paid by the General.

Hammett said no more as we moved to my car and I opened the door.

"Never been in one of these," he said as he climbed in.

"You're in for a rare treat," I said.

We drove past Al, who waved at us with the fist that still clutched the quarters.

"You can get two bottles for that money in San Francisco or Spokane, if you know where to go," Hammett said, looking straight ahead. "And I know where to go."

"Where can I take you?" I asked. "And why did you follow me?"

"I'm staying in the Kingston on Beverly," Hammett answered. "Dr. Minck gave you the right information. Last week I went to the Whitehall Street induction center in New York City and attempted to enlist. They turned me down. No surprise. I'm forty-eight years old. I've drunk as much or more than your friend Zanzibar. My lungs are shot from tuberculosis. The scars showed in my X-rays. Hell, I'm a disabled World War I veteran. I convinced them that I had stopped smoking and drinking, which I have, and that my lungs are all right, but they rejected me because of the teeth. So . . ."

"You got on a plane, came to Los Angeles and picked the first dentist you ran into," I said, heading west toward Sunset. "You couldn't do it in New York?"

"Something like that," he agreed. "There's a woman in New York who might succeed in talking me out of this. I wanted to get as far from New York as possible. When I go back I'll need to be sober, have a healthy mouth and be inductable before I have to deal with Lillian."

"You could do better than Sheldon Minck," I said.

"Perhaps, but I could also do worse," he said. "I think I picked him because his was the only package I have ever encountered which included a dental office and private investigation agency, and I've encountered some strange businesses."

"And you need a private investigator?" I asked.

"No," he said. "I've been in the business."

"I know," I said. "Then . . ."

"Let's say I'm offering my services for a few days while Dr. Minck gets rid of some teeth and gives my mouth some semblance of health, at least cosmetic semblance."

He paused to let me take it in, and it was a lot to take in. The man at my side had written stories, books, movies. I'd seen the movies, read the books.

"I'm no Sam Spade," I said.

"No one is, quite," he said. "He's the devil's version of me at my worst and best."

"And I'm no Continental operative, though I probably look more like him," I went on.

Hammett inspected me.

"No, Jimmy Wright, a Pink back in Baltimore, came the closest," Hammett said.

"So what is it? You want me to play Nora to your Nick?"

"I considered spending a few days with my wife and daughters," he said, "but it's been too long and . . . if I go back to the hotel I'm likely to start smoking and remembering what a drink or two can do to get you through elastic hours. I don't write anymore, not real stuff. If I can keep busy for two or three days and get back to New York sober and in reasonable shape, I can talk them into letting me enlist. The plain truth is that the U.S. Army in the middle of its worst war may be the only thing that can save my life. There's an irony there that doesn't escape me."

I looked his way. He looked out the window.

"Forget it. It was a bad idea," he finally said. "A whim. I don't usually go for them."

"Wait a minute," I came back, assuming he was talking about giving me a hand and not about joining the army. "I could use some help on a case. Just follow-up and tracing."

"That's how I made my living," he said. "I've been beaten, clubbed, knifed and shot at. I finally gave it up and turned to writing full time when I got my skull dented on a case, couldn't stop coughing blood and almost lost touch with what passes for the real world. Dent's still there in the noggin to remind me."

"What the hell," I said. "No salary and the food's on me. Might even get Shelly to give you a discount."

"No need," he said. "I may be emotionally and physically bent but I'm far from financially broke."

3

ndrew Lansing did not live in the poverty belt of Los Angeles County. Life would have been much easier if he had. No, Andrew Lansing lived in an enclosed Pacific Palisades development with a high gate, a guard and, probably, large dogs with big teeth. It made one wonder where Andrew Lansing got his money before he ran off with MacArthur's political war chest.

I drove past the driveway and came to a stop a block beyond. I laid out the situation for Hammett and told him only what I had to tell him, that I had to get through that gate, find the house of Andrew Lansing, and get any information I could on where he might be.

"Lansing's run off with some money, a lot of money," I said. "And some papers that are worth something, particularly to the wrong people."

Hammett nodded, stone cold, and said, "Come back to the gate in five minutes. They'll let you through and we can drive up to Lansing's house."

"You're sure about that?" I said.

"Reasonably," he said.

"What'll you say?"

"I'll improvise," he said, getting out of the car.

I watched him walk back toward the gate in my rearview mirror. As he walked, he stood straighter. By the time he hit the gate his shoulders were squared. He was into whatever character he had taken on.

I looked at the wristwatch my father had left me. According to the battered timepiece it was two-twenty. The watch always ran, but no matter how many times I reset it, it had a will of its own. I flipped on the radio and found Vic and Sade on KNX, which meant it was after ten-thirty. Uncle Fletcher was telling Sade that it was time for a family reunion, and Sade was telling Uncle Fletcher that Vic would be against it. Just then Rush came in excitedly claiming that the Gooch cat was stuck in the mailbox.

I figured five minutes had passed. I made a U-turn and headed back to the iron gate where Hammett, animated and looking a lot healthier than he had ten minutes earlier, stood chatting with one of two gray-uniformed guards. Hammett was nodding sympathetically. He spotted me and waved me forward. I rolled down the window.

"Floyd," he said. "Mr. Lansing's house is number six just beyond the far turn at the left." He handed me a key. "You go get started and I'll join you in a while. Arthur and I have a few things to talk about. Arthur was in the Rainbow Division during the last war."

"That a fact?" I said, looking at Arthur, a potato of a man. He nodded in agreement.

I drove on before the other guard, who was more the celery type, started to get suspicious. Number six was easy to find, a white stone building surrounded by trees with a good view of the ocean through a clump of trees. The next house was about thirty yards down the road, which looked recently paved. I parked in front of the house, walked to the door and opened it with the key Hammett had handed me. I left the door unlocked so Hammett could get in.

The house was dark. The drapes and curtains in every room had been closed. The furniture was all new, modern stuff with lots of chrome. The walls in the living room were dark wood, with paintings of women tastefully spaced along them.

The women looked fine. I didn't care much for the furniture. The house wasn't big but it wasn't small either. I moved through the first floor, checking the living room, dining room and kitchen. I opened drawers, turned them upside down, turned the paintings around, unscrewed the bases of the lamps so I could look inside and, in general, did a pretty thorough job. Major Castle and his men had apparently done a good job of going over the place and putting everything back. The only clear sign of someone else having gone over the place was the fact that the screws in the bases of the lamps came out too easily, as if someone had recently turned them.

I kept looking. The refrigerator was well stocked. Fancy cheeses, wine, juices, eggs. I opened everything and pulled the ice cube trays out to be sure nothing was in them but ice. The shelves were filled. I pulled down boxes, opened them, and sampled the contents of a jar of honeyed wheat germ. I had climbed up on the sink and was considering an assault on a jar of semi-stale cookies on a high shelf when I heard the front door open.

Hammett came into the kitchen and looked up at me. His cheeks had some color in them and he seemed pleased with himself.

"Not the first rube I've caught with his hand in the cookie jar," he said.

"They're stale—macaroons. Want one?" I said, pushing the jar back and easing my way down with two macaroons in hand.

"No, thanks," he said, brushing back his white hair. "Someone wanted privacy in here the last few days."

"The drawn curtains," I said.

"Drapes, shades," he said, looking around. "They're usually open. You can see where the sun bleached out the rug in the front room."

I bit off a corner of macaroon and asked him what he had told the guards.

"Two ways to go," he said, crouching to look up at the underside of the kitchen table. "Blend in and get lost or make the lie big. We didn't have time to blend. I told him I was Lansing's uncle, that I had recently bought a home down the road, that I had just been hired as the attorney for the Los Angeles Police Department and that I was supposed to meet my nephew here at eleven to discuss redecorating his home."

"And who am I?" I asked, looking for a place to dump the cookie.

"Interior decorator," he said. "Your car is being repaired and you're using your son's for the day."

"And they bought it?" I marveled, locating the garbage can under the sink. There was garbage in it, including a few opened envelopes.

"I told them that Andrew would be back soon and that they should tell him I'm here as soon as he arrives," Hammett went on while turning over the kitchen chairs and checking their bottoms. "I hinted strongly to Arthur that my department was in need of reliable men like him, men with a military background. Arthur has reason to expect a call in the near future from a Lieutenant Flynn."

I was used to putting my hands in garbage. This time it wasn't too bad except for the coffee grounds. The envelopes were all from bills.

I led the way back to the staircase and headed up. Something moved in one of the rooms above. All the doors were closed. I pointed to a door directly in front of us at the top of the stairs. Hammett nodded in agreement. We took our time going up the final five steps. At the top of the landing, Hammett put his hand under his jacket and came out with his finger pointed and thumb up in imitation of a gun. I shook my head no. Hammett nodded and looked around. He quickly pulled a white handkerchief out of his pocket and quietly placed a handful of coins in the center of it. He twisted the handkerchief, tied the end and demonstrated a reasonably good homemade blackjack. The entire project had taken him no more than ten seconds.

"I always carry a pocketful of coins for special occasions like this," Hammett explained.

When he was ready I moved to one side of the door and he stood at the other with his weighted handkerchief in hand. I reached for the handle, twisted it quickly and pushed the door open hard. Hammett was at my side in the nearly darkened room. Thin slits of sun crept around the closed curtains. Someone was there. We could both hear him.

I found the light switch, hit it and turned, knowing that whatever was in there had spent time adjusting to the darkness but would be vulnerable to a shock of sudden light. The bedroom was empty. The bed was unmade. Pillows on the floor, blanket in a heap.

I pointed to the floor under the bed. Hammett nodded no and pointed to a closed door, a closet or bathroom. We held our breath and I heard a slight movement beyond the door. Whoever was in there had heard me open the door, had probably heard us come in the house. He or they either didn't have a gun or they did and thought we were armed.

I took four steps to the closed door, pulled it open, a dark screeching ball leapt at my face. I threw up my hands and saw Hammett step forward and swing his loaded handerchief at a naked man just inside the door. I went tumbling backward and tripped on one of the pillows on the floor. The dark ball had hit my face, scratching my cheek and filling my nose, mouth and eyes with something soft and furry.

I grabbed the screeching creature and pushed it away. The cat flew into the corner, landed on its feet and tore out of the room. I tried to get up to help Hammett with the man in the bathroom, but he didn't need help. The man, wearing nothing but a pair of glasses, was on his back on the tiles of the bathroom floor.

"He's dead," Hammett said looking at the body.

"You killed him with a handful of nickels and dimes?"

"Nickels and dimes don't make holes in a man's chest," Hammett said. "I dented the skull of a corpse."

I got up, touched the claw scratch on my cheek and moved to Hammett's side to look down at the body. The corpse looked surprised. He lay dead and naked, staring at the ceiling.

"Cat must have been locked in with him," Hammett said, kneeling next to the body. "I'd say he's been dead less than eight hours."

"I'd say I agree."

"Someone propped him against the wall," said Hammett, removing the glasses from the corpse and dropping them in his pocket. "Rigor straightened him. Damned odd. Only seen one standing corpse. That was back in Omaha, a second-story man named Booster Eddie Simms. Booster Eddie had a wild left eye. Damned thing danced all around the place. Couldn't carry on a serious conversation with Eddie because of that eye. This Lansing?"

Hammett was having a hell of a good time.

"No," I said. "It's probably his roommate, Hower."

Hammett turned back into the bedroom while I examined the body. Four bullet holes, lots of dried blood. Lots of blood on the floor, the walls, the sink. The mirror was bullet-hole cracked.

"It's Hower," Hammett said behind me. "Pants and wallet here. Sixty bucks. No robbery."

"No robbery," I agreed stepping back out of the bathroom and trying to slow down the thoughts. Thought one: Castle and his men came in. Hower was taking a shower. Castle or one of his men ran into him and shot him. Okay. What did that mean? Why didn't Castle just make it look like a murder during a breaking and entering? Leave the place a mess, take the money from the wallet? Thought two: Castle, maybe with or without MacArthur's knowing it, had set me up, sent me here to take the count for Hower's murder. I didn't like that thought. Thought three: Lansing killed Hower. Why? I don't know. Whatever happened, Lansing was gone and Hammett and I were going to be identified by Arthur the gatekeeper and his partner.

Hammett was sitting on the unmade bed smoothing his thin mustache with the nail of his nicotine-stained right thumb.

"Let's get the hell out of here," I said.

"Let's finish what we started," he said. "No one's going to bother us for at least an hour. If you had something bigger than a Crosley, we might consider getting the body out of here. That would buy us time."

"And obstruct justice," I said.

"Obstruct the law," Hammett corrected, getting up. "The law and justice are not always the same. All right. We leave the body."

For the next twenty minutes we searched. I checked the second bedroom, the closets. He took the dead man's room and the small attic. I could swear he was humming as we looked. He was humming and I was sweating.

Twenty minutes later we were about ready to call it a wasted morning. We went down the stairs and I reached for the door. From the kitchen, the cat let out a wild wail. Hammett and I looked at each other and moved quickly back into the kitchen.

"I didn't see any cat food," I said.

"They probably fed him table food, but I don't see a bowl."

I found a can of tuna and an opener and opened the can while the ball of orange and white fur rubbed against my leg. Hammet filled a bowl with water.

When the smell of the tuna hit the cat, he meowed, turned his head and dashed for a space next to the refrigerator. I followed him and found him pushing against the door of a low wooden cabinet. I opened the cabinet door. Inside was a supply of canned cat food. When I picked up the top can, the stack toppled. I shoved the cans back in the cabinet and noticed the loose board. I used a kitchen knife to pry the board up and found a small cloth bag.

Hammett put the bowl of water next to the cat and went with me to the kitchen table where I opened the bag and dumped its contents. There were three stacks of money, neatly wrapped and taped, and there were four letters—all from a Mr. Gerald Pintacki in Angel Springs. Each letter contained only one word. The first, postmarked July 6, read: "Yes." The second, postmarked August 2, read: "Soon." The third, postmarked August 29, read: "Ready." The fourth, postmarked September 1, read: "Saturday."

I tucked the letters in the inside pocket of my jacket. The hungry cat had gulped down the can of tuna and was rubbing against my leg and purring for more.

Hammett leaned over, picked up the cat and tucked it under his arm.

"We'll take him," he said, "Who knows when he'll eat next if we don't."

I considered a protest but let it drop. I had other things to think about. "Fine," I said.

"Peters," Hammett said. "This hungry cat was locked in a room with a bloody corpse. Did you see a mark on that body besides the bullet holes? This is a cat of principle, a cat to be admired."

"I love him," I said. "Now let's go."

Hammett stopped at the front closet near the door. We'd both been through it but he opened it again, rummaged around with his free hand and came up with a blue baseball cap. He handed it to me.

"Put it on," he said.

I put it on and he handed me the glasses he had taken from the dead man upstairs. I put them on too. I could see, but not very well.

"Look over the tops and let them drop on your nose," he advised. "The scratch is a problem."

I touched the tender line under my left eye where the cat had left his mark.

"I'll try to maneuver Arthur and his friend to right side of the car so they won't see it," Hammett went on. "Did something like that with Tiffany Jack Rourke in Butterfield, Kansas. Corrupt little town. Lucky to get out with our lives."

"What about you?" I asked. "What's your disguise?"

"Too late for that. He's already had a good look at me. Besides, you live in this town," he said. "If things go right, I'll be out of California and in the army in less than a week. I know how to stay out of sight for a few days. I have another idea or two. Let's go."

He stepped forward, stroking the cat, and waited for me to open the door. I did, pulled the baseball cap forward and hurried to the car, the glasses low on my nose so I could see over them.

Hammett got in the Crosley next to me and we headed for the gate. Arthur and his buddy were standing around and talking. Both were on the passenger side of the car as we approached.

"Stop right in the driveway," he whispered, putting the cat on the floor.

I stopped, pushed the glasses up in front of my eyes and waited while Hammett leaned out of the open window.

"Arthur," he called. "My nephew didn't show up and I've got to get to a meeting. Tell him I'll call him tonight, and don't you forget you'll be getting a call from my assistant, Ryan."

"I won't forget, Mr. Lansing," Arthur said amiably.

"And Arthur," he went on. "Do you know a pair of men living near my nephew, brothers, named Samuels or Lemuel, something like that?"

"Can't say I do," said Arthur, looking puzzled.

"Odd," sighed Hammett. "They stopped by. One tall older man, gray hair, thin, about six-two, old suit. The other fat, bald?"

"Doesn't sound familiar to me, Mr. Lansing. You know these guys, Bill?"

Bill didn't know these guys. Hammett waved and smiled and whispered for me to drive on. I drove about ten yards slowly, pushed the glasses away from my eyes and stepped on the gas. A block later I took off the glasses and threw the cap behind the driver's seat.

"That will give the police two descriptions of a pair of men seen lurking near Lansing's house," said Hammett. "Let's find a phone and give them a third."

We stopped at a gas station on Washington Boulevard just off the highway. While a kid who looked like he was six filled the Crosley, Hammett and I went into the station. The cat stayed in the car, hiding under the driver's seat.

"I'm feeling better already," Hammett said with a grin, breathing in the slightly smoggy air.

There was a phone in the station. It was reasonably private but I stood watch while Hammett called the Pacific Palisades police. His Italian accent was the best I'd heard.

"Police?" he asked. "My name is Manfriedo and I justa see two men coming out of this house near where I work. They look like they in one bigga hurry and my partner, he say, 'No one home at Mr. Andrew Lansing's house. Who they?' So I calla you. I think maybe they rob the place."

Hammett paused, automatically reached into his jacket pocket where he probably usually kept his cigarettes, changed his mind and nodded his head.

"Sure. One man he young like my son Gino who's fighting the Nazis somewhere. I don't know. About thirty maybe. Yellow hair, almost white. Thin man. The other guy? He's tall, maybe six foot, built like a wrestler. Nose like a bird. That's all I see. No, wait. They got in one of those little cars like Willie the Milkman has, a Hillman, a brown Hillman. Sure . . ." He paused and began to scratch the mouthpiece of the phone with his fingernails. "Something's wrong with thisa phone. I call you back after work if I get a chance. You check on Mr. Lansing's house. I'm worried he's . . ." And Hammett hung up.

"Hungry?" I asked.

"Starved," Hammett said, rubbing his long fingers together.

I paid the kid and we got back in the car, drove up Sunset to Pico and headed east. We stopped for lunch at a place Hammett knew called Al Sandy's on La Cienega. Hammett tucked the cat under his arm and led the way into the restaurant. It was a little late for lunch so the place wasn't crowded. It would have taken a lot of people to fill Al Sandy's. The place was long, narrow and dark with a low ceiling that sagged every few feet. The tables were covered with red and white checked tablecloths, some of them reasonably clean.

In the farthest corner, a group of old men were arguing in a language that sounded like it might be Greek. The waiter, gray haired and wearing a white apron over his round belly, nodded at Hammett and continued to chew something the size of a baseball.

"What'll it be, sports?" the waiter asked as we sat.

"Anarchy," said Hammett, putting the cat on the table.

"I don't recommend it," said the waiter. "How about the salad, fried squid, a couple glasses of wine and some baklava instead?"

Hammett shrugged and nodded. "And the same for the cat."

The waiter nodded and gulped down some of his baseball. He looked me over, decided he didn't need my opinion, and wandered slowly toward the short-order window, behind which stood a dark, thin, sweating man in an undershirt and white chef's toque.

"Well?" Hammett said when the waiter was gone.

"I go to Angel Springs," I said.

"I know somebody there," Hammett said, absently petting the cat, which closed its eyes in delight. "Might be able to open a door or two."

"Okay, *we* go to Angel Springs," I amended as the waiter brought a basket of bread and glasses of red wine. Hammett poured his wine into his butter saucer and let the cat drink it. I didn't see how the wine could hurt the cat, or Hammett for that matter. It had been watered to the point where you could brush your teeth with it.

The fried squid was good and the wine deceptive. I was feeling a little sleepy when the small cups of black tar came and woke me up.

"You want to drive?" I asked, after I had paid the check and we headed for the door, cat purring under Hammett's arm.

"I don't drive," he said, waving at the waiter, who let his eyes droop to let us know what a pleasure it had been to serve us. "Had an accident when I was driving a bus during the war in '18. Some people got hurt. I haven't been behind a wheel since."

"Suit yourself," I said, and he did.

I drove him back to his room in the Kingston Hotel on Beverly. He explained that he usually stayed at the Beverly Hills Hotel, where he had run up some bills that made the maids blush, but the Kingston was a better place to keep a low profile. I promised to be back for him in and hour or so. I had a few places to go before I went to Mrs. Plaut's and packed a change of underwear. Hammett took the cat.

I lied about the underwear. I had nothing to pack but I did want to see Ann. I figured I could just make it to her new apartment in Culver City and back in an hour. I was right, but there were a few things I hadn't counted on. One of them was my brother, Phil.

4

Ann's apartment was one of eight facing a courtyard with a little fish pond in the middle. I took a quick look at the fish. They were gold and black, big-eyed and gulping. The pond looked like it could use a cleaning. The red brick courtyard itself was filled with small, thick-stemmed plants with big leaves. It was like thousands of other little places in California cities, trying to look tropical instead of small and cluttered.

Ann had come down fast. This wasn't even as nice as the apartment complex she had lived in before she married Ralph and moved to Santa Monica.

Number seven was tucked into a corner. I knocked at the door, heart pounding, half hoping she wouldn't be home. But she was.

"Toby," she said, opening the door with a smile. Then she realized what she had done, took back the smile and went politely sober.

She looked like Ann: dark, full-bodied, a light green dress. Her hair was naturally curly and black and barely touched her shoulders. Her body was ample, and her lips pink without makeup.

"Ann," I said. "Just stopped by to see if you needed . . ."

"What I need I'll get on my own, thanks," she said.

I didn't go away and she was too polite to close the door on me, though there were times in the past when she had managed to overcome such civility.

"You want to come in," she said, her hand still on the door, her fingernails red, catching the afternoon sun. Ann had class.

"For a minute," I said. "I'm on my way out of town, Angel Springs, on a case."

She stepped back and let me enter. The place was small. I could see beyond the living room to a small bedroom and a kitchen–dining room on the left. Her house in Santa Monica on the beach had five bedrooms, a servant's quarters and a bathroom that would have held this entire apartment with room left over for a volleyball court.

I recognized some of the English-style furniture from her old house.

"Can I sit?" I asked.

"I don't think so," she said with a wary and weary smile, looking at the gold watch on her left wrist. "I don't think you have it in you. But you may. I'll have to leave in about ten minutes. I've got a job interview with Republic Airlines at four."

"You look voluptuous," I said, sitting on a bowlegged chair.

"I'm sagging, Toby," she said, sitting across from me on another bowlegged chair. She didn't offer me anything to drink.

"Never," I said.

"I'm almost forty-five," she said, playing with the bracelet on her wrist. "My husband died leaving me nothing and I have to go back to work. I'm a tired woman, Toby. Why don't you just stop doing this and go chase someone who doesn't know your underwear size and the way you snore when you don't sleep on your left side?"

"How much did you clear for the house?" I asked, ignoring her question.

Ann crossed her legs and looked down at her nails.

"Enough to put away a little. We owed a lot on it."

"You don't look tired. You look like a twenty-two-year-old right out of college and ready to enjoy her first apartment and new job," I said. "You just think you should feel tired and depressed."

Ann shrugged, got up and straightened her dress.

"I need this job, Toby," she said. "This dress, from J. J. Haggarty's, complete with peplum, drapes and pleats, cost me $49.95. The shoes, Peacock's, also from Haggarty, suede pumps, cost $12.95. I need the job to pay for the clothes and I need the clothes to get the job."

She adjusted a little green hat, the price of which she hadn't quoted, checked herself in a mirror near the door and sighed.

"Ralph wasn't worth faking it for, Annie," I said, standing.

"You didn't know him," she said.

"Well enough," I answered. "You want to spend an hour in bed? No, forget I asked that. I couldn't help it. It came over me. You look so . . ."

"Voluptuous," she completed with a grin and a shake of the head. "Toby, the gravy's in the navy. There are eight women to every man and most of the men still around aren't carrying their weight. Even at your age you don't have to chase an ex-wife who knows what your socks will smell like if you take off your shoes."

"You always had a way with words, Ann," I said. "I don't want war widows and riveters."

"I've got to go, Toby," she said, looking at her watch again. "Next time, wait for a formal invitation. It's not that I'm ungrateful for what you did when Ralph died, but . . ."

"One question and I'm gone," I said as she picked up her purse from a chair near the door.

"Ask it and go," she said.

"You need a ride?"

"No," she said. "I still have Ralph's car. Now . . ."

"That wasn't the real question I want to ask," I jumped in as she opened the door. "Honest answer. Wouldn't you like to feel our bodies together again?"

"Honest answer?" she asked, looking at me with shiny brown eyes as big as the dials on an upright Philco radio. "Yes, I would. There were things you were very good at, Tobias. Very good. And it felt good, feels good, to know you want me, but I'm not going to start getting used to you dropping in when you want to, getting to depend on you again, getting disappointed again, shopping for your cereal, listening to your bizarre excuses. You are the oldest twelve-year-old in California. If I wanted children, I would have had them with you."

"I guess that means . . ." I began.

"I'll think about it, but not very hard," she said, opening the door for me to leave. I could smell her perfume as we moved to the door and out. I didn't smile, just stepped past her into the courtyard as she locked the door behind us.

"Nice fish," I said, looking at the pond.

"Building manager says there were more," she said, looking at me. "But one of the tenants threw in a small fish he caught at Lake Arrowhead. It ate its way through the smaller fish and had downed two big ones when the manager pulled him out."

"Moral?" I asked.

"Don't throw odd fish in with the domestic ones," she said. She turned and walked down the red brick path, past a green elephant-eared plant and into the late afternoon. I didn't follow, didn't say anything. I made the mistake of going back to the pond to look at the fish.

They swam in odd patterns, looking for something to eat or be eaten by. Black and gold splashes of paint with tails that . . .

"Fish belong in soup," came a familiar voice behind me.

I played it right. I didn't turn, just kept looking at a big gold one with bulging eyes and a mouth that opened and closed over slightly brackish water.

"Fish are fascinating," I said.

"Why?" asked Lieutenant Steve Seidman of the Los Angeles Police Department.

"You need a soul to understand, Lieutenant," I said, turning to him with a sigh.

"That explains it," he said flatly. There was no expression on his pale skeleton face. For years there had been rumors that Seidman had a rare disease and would soon be gone, but other cops faded and died around him and Seidman went on, a pale shadow beside his boss, my brother, Captain Phil Pevsner of the Wilshire District.

"What we have here is one hell of a coincidence," I said. "Or . . ."

"Phil wants to see you," he said, looking at the fish but seeing nothing that interested him.

"Should I ask?"

"I would," he said.

"Right. Why does he want to see me?"

"Fellow named Hower got himself killed down in Pacific

Palisades. Found the body about an hour ago," Seidman explained. "We got a call about the same time suggesting that you might know something about it."

"And my brother had you . . ."

"And four other detectives," he interjected.

". . . come out looking for me. You got lucky."

"No," said Seidman. "Phil called people you know and found out that Ann got back to town today. He figured you'd come here looking for her. Said you couldn't stay away from her."

"Betrayed by love," I said.

"I wouldn't know anything about that," he said. "I've been a cop all my life. Let's go."

And we went. Seidman trusted me enough to let me drive my Crosley ahead of him. We got to the Wilshire Station in fifteen minutes, bucking the traffic. The Wilshire had been the hotbed of police activity back in 1923 when my brother Phil joined the force. Phil had come in during Prohibition when the department was at its most corrupt. He became a cop the same month the city fathers appointed August Vollmer, the father of police science, to a one-year term to clean up the L.A.P.D. Vollmer, a clean-living police chief from Berkeley, got nowhere, and when his term was about to expire in September of 1924, billboards began to appear all over the city, saying: "THE FIRST OF SEPTEMBER WILL BE THE LAST OF AUGUST." And it was. I remember seeing the signs and asking Phil what they meant. I remember he rapped me in the head and told me to shut up.

I parked in a space on the street and met Seidman in the lobby. The desk sergeant was a young balding guy named Rashkow who'd had his brains shaken and his left leg peppered with shrapnel defending some small island in the Pacific a year before. He was back now and doing desk duty.

I waved at him and he waved back. Rashkow was busy with an angry little woman in a cloth coat and an enormous fat man with a baby face. The fat man was rocking from one foot to the other like a kid who had wet his diaper.

"Lindsey," Rashkow was saying, "you were told that you couldn't sit on Mrs. Wiskler's dogs, now weren't you?"

Seidman let me lead the way up the narrow dark stairway and around to the left, past the squad room, to my brother's office. I knocked and went in when Phil grunted. Seidman stayed outside.

"I'm in a good mood, Toby," Phil said, looking up at me from his desk. He was clearly packing. There were two cardboard boxes on his desk, both filled. The drawers of his desk were open. His tie was open wide and he looked at me and ran his thick right hand through his short steely gray hair. Phil pulled his gut in and stood up with a deep sigh.

"That's good, Phil," I said. "You're moving?"

"Back to the old office," he said, face pink. "No more administration. I'll have a case load, regular squad. No more being nice to old ladies and storekeepers."

"Back to head bashing," I said. "Couldn't happen to a nicer guy."

"I told you," Phil said, pointing a finger at me. "I am in a good mood. Don't provoke me. And before you can ask, Ruth is fine. Nate and Dave and Lucy are fine. Now, what's going on with this crap in Pacific Palisades. Why'd they call me?"

"I . . ."

"I think we've got a pair of gatekeepers who can identify you," he cut in. "So don't give me any of your cockeyed stories."

"I didn't kill him," I said. "I just found the body."

"I know that," Phil said, emptying a drawer into one of the boxes. Paper clips, broken pencils and pieces of paper fluttered. Some of it got into the box. "Medical examiner just called. Hower was killed last night. You didn't get there till this morning. What the hell were you doing there? Who was the guy you were with? Why is someone calling me and trying to nail you with murder one?"

"I'm on a case," I said. "Missing wife. Thought she might be with Hower. Faked my way in and found his body. So I got the hell out."

Phil grunted and opened another drawer before he spoke.

"Hower didn't like wives or girls," Phil said. "He liked husbands and boys. And who was with you?"

"An ex-Pink I hired to give me a hand, name's Dain."

Phil paused again and pursed his lips.

"Two men on one case. Husband must have a few bucks."

"He's all right," I said.

"Bullshit," said Phil gently, stretching the words out to fill the room. "We've got a murder and a missing roommate named Lansing. We've got a call trying to nail you. Any idea of who that call might be from?"

"None," I said. "Some people don't like me."

"Impossible," Phil said, shaking his head. "Not like my little brother?"

"Incredible," I agreed, "but sadly true."

"See these two boxes?" Phil said, picking up the nearest one.

I had a feeling we were going to play a game I didn't like. My nose had been broken three times, twice by Phil. Phil had been known to use whatever he had in his hands to attack lawbreakers and his brother. Phil had no imagination. The shortest distance to make a point was right through your head.

"I see it, Phil," I said.

"Good," said Phil. He lifted the box and hurled it over the desk toward my head. I ducked as it grazed my shoulder and slammed against the wall.

Seidman stuck his head in, no expression on his face. He looked around, saw the mess and Phil's red face, understood and closed the door.

"Who's going to clean that up, Toby?" he said, trying to control himself.

"I'll be happy to help, Phil," I said.

"Thanks," he said, and hurled the second cardboard box at me. This one was heavier and I wasn't ready for it. It caught me in the chest and fell at my feet, breaking open like a ripe piñata. I had a great remark on my lips but I couldn't catch my breath.

"Have a seat. Tell me what happened and we'll both clean up. What do you say?" He slammed his now-empty drawers closed.

I nodded, unable to speak, and sat in one of the two battered wooden chairs across from Phil's desk.

There was a knock at the door and a tall, thin man with a sad face stepped in carrying a large box in his arms. He looked at the mess on the floor, Phil's red face, and me sitting and trying to breathe.

"I thought you'd be moved out by now," the sad man said.

"A little accident, Captain," Phil said. "My brother's helping me clean it up."

"Can I just leave this here and come back later?" he asked.

"Sure thing," Phil said amiably.

The tall man put the box on the second chair and had second thoughts. "Maybe I'll just take it with me," he said.

"It'll be safe here," Phil said.

I shook my head no. The new Captain looked uncertain, but he left the box and headed for the door.

"I can't tell you, Phil," I panted. "I've got a client who . . . I just can't tell you. You can throw boxes, throw me, have a heart attack, break my fingers . . . Wait, I'm not giving you any more ideas. I just can't tell you."

Phil moved around the desk and opened his tie even more. The shirt under his open jacket was stained with sweat.

"I want the son of a bitch who called me and said you did it," he said.

"Brotherly love," I said, sitting up as well as I could. I didn't think any ribs were broken.

"The case isn't mine," he said. "It belongs to Pacific Palisades, but this . . . this . . ."

"Very bad person," I suggested.

"Asshole," Phil continued, rubbing his hands together, "wants you in it, me in it, wants to jerk me around. I don't like being jerked around, Toby."

"That's not new information for me, Phil," I said, trying to get up.

Phil reached over to help me.

"I don't like it when you jerk me around especially, Toby," he said. "I've had half a century of it. You're breathing funny. Did you break a rib?"

"Did I break a rib?" I asked, letting him get me to my feet while I demonstrated a hell of a lot more pain than I felt. "You threw the box at me."

"Let's not play with words," Phil said.

"You going to finish the job, throw me in the tank, invite me for dinner or let me go?" I asked.

"How many days do you want before I come back at you?" he asked.

"Four," I said.

"Three," he countered. "Three and I get answers or you go in the tank."

"Three days," I agreed. "I'll give you a hand with this mess."

"Get out," Phil said with a wave. "You ruined my mood. I'll do it myself."

"I've got something to improve your disposition. You want a cat?" I asked from the door. "Kids love cats."

Phil was looking at the mess on the floor and leaning against his desk, his hands folded in front of him.

"I ate cats when I was in the army, in the trenches," he said. "I ate worse than cats. I can't think of them as pets for kids. I can only think of them as stringy food."

"The good old days in the Rainbow Division," I said.

"Three days," he said, and I was out the door and into the hall.

"He's in a good mood or you'd be in the tank or the hospital," Seidman said, walking with me to the stairway.

"Well, I know he charmed me," I said. "You know where to find me."

"I know how to find you," Seidman corrected.

I arrived at Hammett's hotel on Beverly almost an hour late. He was sitting in the lobby, small overnight case at his feet, cat in his lap. A girl, young, pretty, blonde, made up and no more than twenty, was leaning over Hammett and admiring the cat.

"He's cute," she said.

As I moved forward, I could see him looking at the girl's breasts as she leaned forward. "How long are you staying at the hotel?" Hammett asked.

"A few days. Till my mother comes up from San Diego to drive me back to school," she said, taking me in as I stepped into the conversation.

"Perhaps we could have dinner tomorrow night, Cindy, and

discuss feline futures," Hammett said softly, looking at her with great sincerity.

"Maybe," she said, blushing. "Might be fun. I've got to go. Bye, kitty."

And off she went. We both watched her head across the lobby and out into the night.

"Hooker," I said.

"No doubt," he agreed. "But I've learned it doesn't hurt to indulge a young girl's fantasies. The cat and I will do our best to entertain Cindy when we get back tomorrow."

Hammett got up, handed me the cat, picked up his overnight case and started across the lobby.

"Don't you want to know why I'm late?" I asked.

"The police or a woman," he said.

"Both," I acknowledged, cradling the cat as we walked. "Someone called saying I'd killed Hower."

"And the police didn't buy it?" he asked as we followed Cindy the Hooker into the night. "Do they know about my being with you?"

"Not yet," I said.

"Right. Then let's go find a killer."

We got into my car and headed east. Hammett went quiet as the Crosley bumped through the Los Angeles evening traffic. He sat with the sleeping cat on his lap and looked out of the window, dreaming. He was wearing a tweed jacket a little too warm for the Southern California afternoon but just right for the desert evening. I had on my Windbreaker and a grim expression.

By the time we hit the highway outside the city, it was getting dark and Hammett was still looking out of the window, rocking with the roll of the road and petting the cat.

"Stop for something?" I asked.

"If you like," he said.

I grunted and found a truck stop with a diner. We sat at the counter and Hammett put the cat in front of us. I ordered a couple of burgers and a Pepsi. Hammett had some soup and a Green River. The cat had his own bowl of artichoke soup and a lot of attentio from a small bull of a waitress in a faded orange uniform, who went mushy over him.

"Cute cat," she said.

Hammett agreed. The place wasn't too crowded. A lone craggy-looking trucker with a gut sat in a corner, eating silently and reading the newspaper. A couple of guys in overalls and boots came in right after us and sat together at the end of the counter. The radio, a little white Arvin, belted out the news. The waitress cooed at the cat.

"A communiqué issued by General MacArthur's headquarters in Australia indicates that a Japanese landing force of seven hundred has now been practically destroyed at Milne Bay in southeastern New Guinea," came the rapid-fire voice of the newscaster.

"You have a friend in Angel Springs," I reminded Hammett.

"I have a friend," he confirmed, drinking his beer. "The trouble with beer is that it is near enough to drinking to keep the memory alive and far enough from it to be a little dissatisfying."

". . . said the Japanese still were held on the north side of the Owen Stanley mountain range about two thousand feet below 'the gap,' which is virtually the only pass trail through the rugged mountains," the newscaster went on.

"Beer is fine with me," I said. "Your buddy in Angel Springs . . ."

"We'll stop and see him," Hammett agreed, watching the plump waitress whisper to the cat. The waitress's name, according to the little name tag on her uniform, was SHEILA.

"I had a cat when I was a kid," she said, looking up at us. "His name was Greenbaum on account of my sister thought he had a Jew nose. You know what I mean?"

"I know exactly what you mean," Hammett said. "You think Jews have funny noses."

"I didn't mean . . ." she said, taking a new interest in our faces in case we had Jew noses. My unaltered nose might have caused her confusion, but the mashed flesh between my eyes and over my mouth had no shape to give an ethnic clue. Hammett's nose was movie-star perfect.

"You didn't think," Hammett corrected her.

"No need to get highbrow on me, mister," the box of a waitress said, straightening up and adjusting her uniform.

"Let it go," I said, finishing my burger.

"You are Jewish, aren't you, Mr. Peters?" Hammett asked.

"I guess," I said.

"Are you offended by Miss Olympia's comment?" Hammett asked, scratching the cat's head.

"It's not worth it," I said.

". . . German tanks, infantry and planes have made a frontal assault on Stalingrad from the west and have forced the Russians back to new defensive positions, according to the Soviet high command," the radio voice went on, in the same tone of panic.

"It's always worth it," Hammett said gently.

"I'm sorry," the waitress said.

"It's okay," I moved in. "I'm finishing this burger and the fries and we're off."

"Guys giving you trouble?" one of the two overalled customers called over to the waitress.

"No trouble," Sheila said. "I just sometimes don't know when to keep my mouth shut."

Hammett pursed his lips and tugged gently at the cat's ear. The cat kept lapping at the soup.

"Just the same," the overalled customer said, getting off his stool. "These guys are giving you trouble."

The man on the radio said that the British and Americans had dropped three thousand tons of bombs on Tobruk and given Rommel something to think about along with the new assault of American tanks.

"No trouble," Sheila said. "No trouble. Just sit down and finish your blue plate, will you?"

But the two men, who looked much bigger when standing, were moving behind me and Hammett. I kept eating the second burger.

"You upset Sheila," one of the men said to us behind our backs.

Hammett looked up from the cat to examine Sheila's face seriously.

"Could be," he finally said.

"We'll just call it our contribution to improved harmony among all the great contributors to the American melting pot," I added.

"Don't play smart with me. I'm not stupid," he said angrily.

"I appreciate the information," Hammett said, downing the last of his beer. "Without it I'd have gone through life in the belief that I'd run into Clifton Fadiman in a diner."

"I'm gonna smash your face," the man behind us said.

"Forget it, for chrissake, will you?" Sheila screeched.

The lone old trucker in the corner went on eating and reading and pretending none of this was happening. The guy on the radio seemed to be getting more and more excited as he ran out of news.

". . . bombers hit Crete . . . U-boats sink two Allied merchant ships . . ."

"Get up," the bigger guy in overalls said to Hammett and me.

In the stainless-steel coffee pot behind the counter I could see the distorted reflection of the two big men, walking ads for how to abuse the products of Oshkosh B'Gosh. They were not only bigger than Hammett and me, they were younger, quite a bit younger.

Hammett looked over at me with a smile, a strand of the white hair curving down his forehead. Before I could return his smile, Hammett threw his elbow back, a sudden, sharp jab. It hit the nearest man, the one who had been doing the talking, just below his chest and just over a rivet on his overalls. The man staggered backward to the sound of Sheila screaming, "No, no, no, you'll get me canned."

The second man, who looked something like a bulldog, put his hand on Hammett's neck as I spun half a turn on my genuine leatherette-covered stool and threw the cat in his face. The man tripped back with a dull bleat as the cat bounced off him. I could see now that the two men had their names neatly sewn over their pockets. The one Hammett had hit, WYLIE, had pulled himself together and was looking for something lethal. He picked up a wooden chair from a nearby table. By now Hammett and I were on our feet, with our backs to the counter. The cat jumped back on the counter and went for the remainder of the soup while we waited for the denimed duo to come at us again. There were cat scratches on the face of Wylie's buddy, CONRAD, and a look on that bloody face that I couldn't figure out. Conrad, panting, saw the chair in Wylie's hands, thought it a great idea, and went for one of his own.

Hammett had the heart, but I didn't think he had the staying power. He coughed a couple of times at my side while Wylie and his friend Conrad moved forward. I wasn't even sure why we were fighting, but I knew there was no sense in pointing this out to the boys. Wylie raised his chair as he came nearer and I was sure he meant to bring it down on whichever one of us was in range. He meant to but he never did. A shot pierced the air and the two men in denim froze and looked at our hands. Neither Hammett nor I had a gun. The cat didn't have one and Sheila, who was blubbering behind the counter, had nothing in her hands but a sopping paper napkin.

We all looked over at the craggy trucker in the corner. He had his newspaper in one hand and a pistol in the other. He was chewing something and looking dyspeptic.

"What the hell?" Wylie began, the chair still raised over his head.

The trucker fired again, into the ceiling.

"I got a load of wheel parts in my rig," the trucker at the table said in a gravely rumble. "And I got three hundred miles to hit before I stop. I want a quiet eat and a simple stomach. And I don't want to see any blood anywhere except in my steak sandwich."

"We can finish . . ." Conrad began.

The trucker fired a third time.

"I got two boys in the army," the old trucker said. "One in North Africa. One in the Pacific. You want fighting? Join up and give my boys a hand."

"I plan to," said Hammett.

"You're near old as me," said the trucker.

"I'd say so."

"You want me to put a hole in these lumps?" the trucker asked.

"Small hole. Slow 'em down a bit."

"No thanks," said Hammett.

Wylie and his friend slowly put the chairs down. They'd learned enough to keep their mouths shut if they didn't want to duck the trucker's bullets.

Sheila was still sobbing behind the counter. The radio newsman was gone. He'd been replaced by Hedda Hopper, who was telling us what a big hit Brian Donlevy was in *Wake Island*.

I dropped two bucks on the counter and Hammett picked up the cat, nodded at the trucker and headed for the door with me behind. We pushed past Wylie and Conrad, whose face was lined with thin red scratches.

"I'll hold these boys a minute or two and send them on their way," the trucker said. "I got the newspaper to finish and I'd like a piece of pie, cherry, if it's close to fresh."

"Coming up," Sheila said, sniffling.

Hammett, the cat and I went into the cool night. The diner door clattered behind us.

"Sometimes it feels damned good to be alive," Hammett said, taking in a deep breath of air.

"Sometimes," I agreed.

5

We hit Angel Springs about three in the morning. Hammett guided me to a house on a street with large, one-story ranch-style houses surrounded by wide, rolling lawns. The house was sprawling, freshly painted and very dark.

"Maybe we should look for a hotel," I said.

"Pudge will be happy to put us up," Hammett said. I was tired. Hammett, who was rod thin and pale, seemed to be full of energy. With me behind him holding the cat, Hammett pushed the button next to the door. A set of chimes sounded and vibrated inside. The cat vibrated in my arms.

No answer.

Hammett pushed the button again. More chimes. The sky was clear and full of stars. No one answered.

"Pudge isn't home," I said. "We should have called."

Hammett pulled out a pocketknife and began to work on the front door.

"You're going to tell me that Pudge won't mind," I said.

"Won't mind at all," Hammett agreed. "I won't even scratch the door."

And he didn't.

The house was empty, if you didn't count the furniture. Hammett, the cat and I prowled, found what looked like a guest room with two beds, and made ourselves reasonably comfortable. We fed the cat with a can of salmon from the pantry, found a cardboard box in a closet and set it up for him in our room. Hammett took a shower. I didn't want one. I stripped down to my underwear and got into one of the beds. I was asleep in four or five minutes. I was awake an hour later. Hammett snored. I got back to sleep before dawn.

I dreamed of vague clowns and cities, greasepaint grins and brick buildings crumbling slowly with people inside. I dreamed that one of the clowns—it might have been my old friend Koko from past dreams and childhood nightmares—removed a cornerstone from one of the buildings, flew above me and lowered the stone on my chest. I caught my breath, wanted to push the acid-smelling stone away, tell him it was a lousy joke, but I couldn't move my arms and then the awful feeling came, that I knew I was dreaming but I couldn't quite wake up, that I might never wake up, that the stone was holding me in an eternal state between sleep and wakefulness. I groaned and opened my eyes. The cat was asleep on my chest, his tail almost brushing my nose. My arms moved and I pushed him away. The cat's claws caught at the blanket and yanked it away from me. I sat up, trying to catch my breath again, my chest still slightly sore from the box Phil had thrown at me at the Wilshire Station, and found a pistol in my face. The man holding the pistol was toothpick thin with red cheeks and thin gray hair. He looked like an angry trout.

"Do not move," he said.

I didn't move. Hammett wasn't in the next bed.

"I . . ." I began.

"Do not speak," he said, holding the gun tightly and moving to a phone on a table near the bed. I needed better leverage and a few more seconds to wake up. The man didn't know how to hold a gun and didn't have enough sense to stay away from me.

"I'm calling the police," he said.

"Are you Pudge?" I asked.

He put down the phone and looked at me with curiosity.

"There are those who call me that," he agreed. "And there was a time when it seemed less ironic. What are you doing in my house? What are you doing in my guest bed? Why do you have a cat?"

Pudge's composure had dropped like a washed-up heavyweight in a mismatch with Joe Louis.

"I need a drink," he said. "Would you like one?"

The gun was still pointed at me but the hand holding it was shaking now.

"Juice, coffee or a Pepsi," I said.

"I don't have those things," Pudge sighed.

"I'll skip the drink," I said. "I think you should point the gun in another direction."

Pudge looked at the gun in his hand as if he were surprised to see it. "Thinking of shooting myself when I heard you bumping around in here, you and the cat. That's why I happened to have the gun. Not used to the damn things anymore. I haven't been well," he said.

"Who has?" I asked, pushing the blanket away from me slowly.

"My wife," said Pudge. "She is disgustingly well. And at the moment is out somewhere playing tennis or golf or something equally distasteful. Have you ever played tennis?"

"No," I said.

"Golf?"

"No."

Pudge smiled, a soft little smile, and the pistol drooped slightly. "They don't make sense to me, either of them," he said. "Can't remember the damned rules. Maybe I never wanted to learn them. Not much I want to remember."

"How about Warmantin's bedpan filled with gin?" Hammett's voice came from the door. He was freshly shaven and fully dressed in dark slacks, white shirt and dark cardigan sweater.

"Sam," Pudge said, pointing the gun at Hammett.

The cat was purring and rubbing against Hammett's legs. He reached down and picked it up.

"Put the gun down, Pudge," he said, moving into the room. "Mr. Peters is a friend. You weren't home last night so we let ourselves in."

Pudge shoved the pistol into his pocket and looked at me with suspicion. "You a publisher, a producer?" he asked. The thin coat of culture in his voice was deserting him fast.

"Private investigator," I said.

"Sam," Pudge said, turning to Hammett. "I thought you were ass high in bread. You didn't have to go back to the dick business. You could have come to me. Money's not my problem."

"Not the money," Hammett said softly. "I'm just helping Mr. Peters out for a few days before I head east and join the army. Let's keep it quiet."

"Lillian?"

"Let's keep it quiet," Hammett repeated even more softly.

Pudge looked at me as I got out of bed and reached for my pants.

"Sam and I go back," he said. "We were in a TB hospital back in '29 or '30. Best goddam time I had in my life. Sam got all the young nurses and we partied in town. Both of us on army disability. Take a look at this."

He opened his robe to reveal a purple scar that ran down the left side of his chest to the navel on his pink belly.

"Verdun," he said. "Some kind of crap got in there before they sewed me up. Crap must have had TB on it. I can't complain. If it didn't happen I wouldn't have met Sam, wouldn't have had the best goddam year of my life. I got money now, Peters. Bought a little farm when I got out of the hospital. What the hell do I know about farms? Goddam dirt. Screwed it up. Then when I was going to pull out and go back to bartending I heard some auto company was planning to build a plant next door. I mortaged my place and bought land all over the place with the bank's money. In less than three months, I sold all the land to the auto company. Made a bundle. Moved here, married Janet of the Jungle. Now I'm not well. Not well at all. Believe me." He pointed to his chest. "The pumps are shutting down. Not much time left and nothing much I want to do with it."

"Sorry," I said.

"Not complaining, just drinking and hoping to remember the good old days, but it's not working. But now that you're here, Sam, hell. Let's have a few drinks and tell Peters about Augie and the blackjack."

"I'm riding the wagon," said Hammett, stroking the cat whose eyes were closed contentedly.

"I'm still a pedestrian," Pudge said with a disappointed grin. He moved to a low wooden cabinet in the corner, opened it and pulled out one of the bottles of amber liquid. "Like to keep the guests supplied. Nunnally stayed here a few weeks back."

Pudge poured himself a drink, straight amber, and leaned against the wall with a sigh as Hammett spoke.

"We've got some questions, Pudge," he said, moving over to his bed and sitting with the cat on his lap.

"Shoot," said Pudge, taking a small sip. I wasn't sure what time it was but it couldn't have been more than nine in the morning. The sun was bright even through the drawn curtains, and Pudge was brightening with it and the drink in his hand.

"Pintacki," Hammett said.

"Pintacki?" Pudge repeated, after puffing out his cheeks. "You mean the nut in the desert? I think his name's Pintacki. No, I'm sure it is."

I put my arm in one sleeve of my semiclean shirt and smiled encouragement at Pudge.

"Tell us," Hammett said.

"Don't know much," Pudge said with a shrug. "Supposedly has a place in the desert just east of town. Doesn't come to town much. Costs a fortune to keep the place up, I hear. Made his money in junk. Word is he wanted to get into the movies, wanted to act, bought his way in for a while, lost a bundle backing a Western, gave up and built this castle in the desert. Supposed to be quite a place out there. Never saw it. Remember Anita with the Irish accent?"

"I remember, Pudge," Hammett said with a smile.

"And Jose . . ." Pudge began and stopped himself. "Sorry, Sam."

"Nothing to be sorry about, Pudge," he said, scratching the cat's head. "I stay in touch with her and the kids. Cops here? How are they?"

"Cops." Pudge shrugged. "Chief's named Spainy. Pisses on the peasants. Kisses the rear end of anyone with ten bucks and a tie. Cops. It's easier here though. Not much of a middle class. Clout's clear."

"How much have you got, clout?" Hammett asked.

Another shrug from Pudge who finished his drink and held his glass in search of some forgotten drop of liquid.

"Don't know for sure," he said. "Probably enough. Janet and I get treated real polite by Spainy."

"Think you could pick up a phone, call this Spainy and have him check out the two guys in the DeSoto parked down the street?" asked Hammett.

I stopped tying my shoes, which needed at least one fresh shoestring, and looked up at Hammett who looked down at me.

"Wylie and Conrad," he said. "From the diner last night."

"How do you figure it?" I asked. "Redneck grudge?"

"Could be," said Hammett, putting the cat gently on the bed, getting up and straightening the creases in his trousers. "But I saw that DeSoto behind us when we left Los Angeles last night."

"Could be lots of things," I said.

"Pudge?" Hammett said. Pudge moved to the phone, picked it up, dialed and pulled himself together.

"Chief Spainy, please," he said in a voice much deeper than the one he had been using a few seconds earlier. "Tell him it's G. Carl Block." Pause. "Janet Block's husband." Another pause. Pudge looked at us with a what-can-you-do expression and then went on. "Chief? Yes, good to talk to you too. How's the campaign going? . . . good . . . excellent. You know you can count on Janet and me for both our votes and a donation . . . as a matter of fact, there is. There's an unfamiliar car parked just down the street from my house and two rather strange-looking characters are sitting in it and . . . yes. A DeSoto . . . well, I'd appreciate it. Thanks."

Pudge hung up and toasted us with his empty glass, eyebrows raised.

"They'll be right over to roust the enemy."

"Thanks, Pudge," Hammett said, getting up and straightening his trousers again.

"My pleasure, Sam, and I have few enough of them," he said, doing for the bottle again. "TB's weakened the system. Taking a long time and going slow at it, but I'm not complaining. It gets me a little sympathy from Janet. Not much, mind you, but a little. Got to settle for what we can get."

"We're all dying, Pudge," said Hammett.

"I'm just doing it a little faster than my friends," said Pudge. "Not complaining, but I kind of like the idea of picking my own time and place. If I could just catch on to a memory I'd feel okay."

"Best we can do is go out with dignity—or having fun," said Hammett. "I haven't made up my mind which one I want. I don't think you can have both."

"More's the pity," said Pudge. "More's the pity."

Enough. I felt like the best friend's friend in a third-rate play. I had nothing to say and the director wasn't coming up with anything for me to do. It didn't matter. I had my own plans. In the distance, a police siren wailed.

"I think I'll go out and greet the pair in the DeSoto before the law gets here," I said.

"Let's," said Hammett.

We left the room with Pudge and closed the cat inside. Pudge wandered off into the house, pistol in one hand, bottle in the other. Hammett and I went out the front door.

"How do you want to do this?" Hammett asked as we stepped into the sun and crossed the lawn, heading straight for the lone car parked on the street right behind my Crosley. The sun was hitting the windshield but I could see two shapes inside.

"Fast," I said, moving quickly before Wylie and Conrad could take off. As it was, they didn't want to take off. They got out of the car to meet us. They were still wearing their overalls and now had an overnight growth of stubble on their faces which didn't improve their bulldog looks. Their identical gray eyes looked puffy and their faces tired. If I had thought they would be thrown by the element of surprise, I was wrong.

"What do you want?" I asked, brilliantly.

Wylie, the shorter of the two, who still stood at least six-three, plunged both hands into the deep pockets of his blue denim overalls and rocked on his heels. I half expected him to say, "Oh shucks," and blush, but he didn't. Instead he came out with a pocketknife which opened with a flick to show a blade that glinted in the bright sun. Behind him Conrad magically produced a short length of pipe.

"It's coming right to us," Wylie said. "And this time no fat gut with a gun is going to save your asses."

"I think they should have had a better plan," I said to Hammett, at my side.

"I don't know. It has its good points," he said in a near whisper. "It's direct, honest and dangerous."

"Those are good points?" I asked, as Wylie and Conrad advanced toward us.

"Usually," he said.

"Yeah."

We stood ready on the lawn. I didn't think much of our odds, but that siren was much closer now. We were giving up too many years and too many pounds, but I had the feeling that Hammett and I knew how to take it better than Wylie and Conrad. If we could give out about as much as we took, we might be able to slow them down till help arrived. It was the best hope I could muster, but I didn't need it. About three blocks down, a car screeched around the corner. Wylie, who was no more than six feet from me, looked over his shoulder, snarled "Shee-it," and jammed his knife back into his pocket. He turned, grabbed Conrad's arm and hurried back to the DeSoto.

"You all write now, you hear?" I said.

"I'll fry your hair," Wylie said, turning over the engine and putting the DeSoto in gear.

"Fry my hair?" I repeated to Hammett, who shuddered.

"He needs a new dialogue writer."

Wylie and Conrad took off after clipping the right rear fender of my Crosley. They hit the nearby corner, turned right and were gone. I ambled over to examine the damage to my car with Hammett right behind.

The fender would need more than work. It would need a suitable burial in an auto graveyard.

The cop car slowed and pulled up behind us in the space just vacated by the grease monkeys from hell.

"Got a problem?" one cop asked, coming out of the driver's seat with a gun in his hand. He wore a neatly cleaned and pressed blue uniform with a blue cap pulled over his forehead in military style.

"The bad guys got away, went around the block," I said. "Blue DeSoto. You might be able to catch up with them."

The first cop, who looked young and solid and wore sunglasses, was joined by an older, heavier version who had come out of the passenger door. He was carrying a shotgun.

"You two mind telling us what you're doing out here?" Cop One asked, with an edge.

"We're guests of Mr. Block," Hammett said. "Two men . . ."

"We can see you're two men," the first cop said with a smirk.

The second cop didn't hold back a grin. He thought his partner was a regular Jerry Colonna.

"Hold it," I said. "Two guys tried to bust our heads last night and then showed up here this morning. Pudge called . . ."

"Pudge?" asked the comic cop. They had spread out, comic cop in the street, sidekick on the lawn. Across the street a door opened and a man in a robe stepped out to watch. He had a gray walrus mustache and a very serious expression.

"Mr. Block's nickname is Pudge," Hammett explained. "The two you're looking for are . . ."

"Maybe right in front of us," said the comic. "This your car?"

"Yeah," I said.

"Don't see many of these in Angel Springs. Don't see many of these that can even make it to Angel Springs."

"God, Barry," the other cop said, shaking his head and smiling, gun still aimed at us.

"Let's make it simple," Hammett said. "Simple enough for Laurel and Hardy here. I suggest we go in and ask Mr. Block."

Barry and his buddy exchanged looks and nodded. I had the feeling that we would have been safer dealing with Wylie and Conrad. The walrus across the street shielded his eyes from the sun to watch us march to Pudge's door.

"Careful," the man across the street called. I couldn't tell who he was warning, us or the cops.

Hammett was reaching for the door when we heard the shot. It came from inside the house, clear, sharp, and only once. Barry shouldered his way past us, his partner aiming his weapon at Hammett, then me, and back again. He wasn't smiling anymore and Barry wasn't making jokes.

Barry turned the door handle and went in, weapon up, hands less than steady.

We followed him. Barry went to his knee on one side of the door. His partner ducked into the living-room doorway on the other side. Hammett and I stood in the hall.

"Police," Barry called into the house.

"Crap," sighed Hammett and stalked down the hallway.

"Stop," called Barry.

Hammett simply threw up his hand in disgust and moved forward with me right behind.

We found Pudge in the kitchen, seated at the table, an empty bottle near his left hand, his pistol in his right. The hole in his temple was deep and almost black. Pudge was smiling as if he had a secret he wasn't going to share. He was right.

6

We spent the morning in the cleanest cell I'd ever been in. If you had to go to jail, Angel Springs was the place to do it. There were only two of us in the cell, Hammett and me. We played poker with an almost new deck of Bicycles at a clean table, and ate a hot meal brought to us on plates.

"I know jokers who'd come up with a dime a night to huddle in a place like this," I said.

"Not bad," Hammett agreed, cutting the cards.

I owed him about thirty bucks by the time an old man in uniform came for us. He opened the cell door and motioned for us to follow him. He stayed about three feet ahead of us, gun bouncing in his holster. We could have taken the weapon, blown his head off and headed back to Los Angeles, but all three of us knew that you didn't do things like that in Angel Springs. We strolled into the outer office of the station past a pair of desks, one empty, the other filled by a dark-haired woman in a blue uniform talking frantically on the phone. She looked up at us and pushed the hair away from her face the way Ann used to do. I smiled at her. She looked through us and went back to her call.

Chief Spainy's office was clean and sunny. The windows were big and freshly washed. The desk was clear and unscratched. Spainy was a bulky little man, in his fifties, with a thick neck. He wore a blue uniform and a tie that choked him and furrowed his throat. He did not look comfortable. He sat behind the desk, hands flat on it, and watched us sit.

"What do you know about rabbits?" he said finally.

"Not much," I said.

"Stupid animals," said Spainy. "Less sense than a chicken, if you can believe that. Less than a fish or frog. I've seen rabbits run right out on Highway 99 and stop dead in the headlights of my jeep, just waiting to get squashed."

"Sounds stupid to me," I said.

"Domestics are even dumber than the wild ones," he went on. "And they aren't so damned friendly. Ever eat rabbit?"

Hammett sat with his hands in his lap, saying nothing, letting me carry the fascinating conversation.

"No," I said.

Spainy shook his head in sympathy for my loss.

"Hassenpfeffer, fried rabbit, rabbit pie, roast rabbit, rabbit cooked in casserole. You take care in raising rabbits, wire-bottom hutches, off the ground. Feed them carefully and nothing tastes better. Nothing—not even a good steak from Kansas or an abalone from up the coast."

He looked at us both to see if we were going to challenge him. We didn't.

"You might guess I raise rabbits," he said, pushing away from his desk and clasping his hands. He grinned. "That would be a good guess, but you might wonder why I'm talking rabbits with you."

"You don't want any trouble," Hammett supplied. "You want to hold your job, raise your rabbits and retire without embarrassment."

"Something like that," Spainy said, losing his grin and not too happy to be upstaged. Upstaging Spainy didn't strike me as a good idea either.

"We don't get people getting shot in our town," he said. "Residents don't like it. And what they don't like I don't like. You know what I like?"

"Rabbits," I said.

"And no trouble," he added. "Now I'll be quiet and you tell me everything there is to tell. I still got the victim's widow to find and some explaining to do for her."

"I'm a private investigator," I said.

"I know that," sighed Spainy. "And you," he said, nodding at

Hammett, "are a big-time writer, *Maltese Falcon, Thin Man,* that kind of stuff. Never read it. Wife does, though. Tell your tale and don't waste time trying to impress the country folk."

"We were staying overnight with Pudge, Mr. Block," said Hammett. "He was depressed. As an autopsy will show, he was dying. He made up a story about two men waiting outside with guns to get us out of the house. Mr. Peters and I went out to look. Your men pulled up, thinking we were the two men, and we heard a shot inside the house."

"Simple so far," said Spainy.

Hammett brushed back his white hair and shrugged.

"But you told my man Barry that a car had just pulled away," said Spainy, shaking his head.

"To protect Mr. Block," I stuck in.

"Dumb-ass story," said Spainy, opening his desk and fishing for something.

"Most true stories are dumb-ass," said Hammett "We were outside with your men when Pudge shot himself. They heard the shot."

Spainy found what he was looking for, a small jar of Postum. "J.V.!" he screamed.

The door to his office opened instantly and the dark, pretty and slightly overweight woman in uniform who reminded me of Ann stepped in, biting her ample lower lip. Spainy threw the small jar to her. She juggled it, managed to keep it from falling and clutched it to her bosom like a back pulling in a pass from Sid Luckman.

"Make a pot of that stuff, will you, J.V.," Spainy said. "You two want some?"

Hammett and I shook our heads.

"Suit yourself," he said, sitting down. "Hate the crap but I've got to drink something since I went off coffee. Hate tea. Don't like cold drinks."

J.V. left with her small jar still clutched tight.

"Could have been an accomplice," Spainy said, returning his gaze to us and raising his eyebrows knowingly. "You could have had someone inside the house firing a gun. Block already murdered.

Or you could have had a record of a shot or set up a gun to go off
with some kind of timer."

"I thought you didn't read detective novels," I said.

"Ah, hell. Jenny leaves 'em laying around. I pick up a few just
to get ideas," he said.

"Maybe we hypnotized Carl," said Hammett. "Made him shoot
himself while we used the police for an alibi."

"Can't make hypnotized people kill themselves," said Spainy,
pointing a finger at Hammett.

"No? Maybe not, but what if they don't know they're killing
themselves?" Hammett went on, warming to the game. "What if
they're told it's a toy gun, or . . ."

". . . a new kind of thing to cut your hair," said Spainy, leaning
forward.

I tried to catch Hammett's eye. Spainy didn't need help in turning
a suicide into a murder and pinning it on us. He needed help in
recognizing it was a suicide.

"That's nuts," I said. "The man shot himself."

Spainy spun around once in his swivel chair, a complete, slow
circle full of thought.

"Seems so, seems so," he agreed. "But I got a feeling something's stirring here I ain't been told. The rabbits are restless. I can
feel it, but suicide's better than murder. People are supposed to
come here, feel good about life, not shoot themselves—but hell,
maybe I shouldn't complain. It's better than murder."

"Most things are," said Hammett.

The phone on Spainy's desk rang. He looked at it with irritation,
looked at the door, looked at us as it rang on, and finally picked it
up with a grunt.

"J.V., I am ensconced," he said, and then put his hand over the
mouthpiece to address us. "Fancy word, huh? You're not dealing
with bumpkins here, Mr. Writer." He removed his hand from the
mouthpiece and listened for a few more seconds before jumping in.
"Yeah . . . okay . . . finish up that Postum and put him on."

Spainy looked at the ceiling, took a deep breath and spoke into
the phone. The folksy Spainy was gone. He could have been a prof
down from Stanford.

"What can I do for you, Mr. Pintacki?" he said into the phone. Hammett and I exchanged glances and Spainy looked up at us as he nodded his head and listened.

"Of course," he said. "I'm sure that can be arranged . . . with the greatest possible dispatch . . . who would? . . . yes, I will . . . Beverly or Salinas . . . glad to help . . . good-bye, sir."

He hung up the phone, looked at it for inspiration, ran his tongue over his lower lip and turned his attention to us.

"Mr. Hammett," he said politely in his Stanford voice. "You are free to go. There's been an obvious misunderstanding and I'm sorry to have inconvenienced you. If you think disciplinary action should be taken against the two officers who brought you in, just tell me."

"I seem to have an influential friend," Hammett said, standing up.

Spainy looked at the phone. "Oh, that," he said with a shrug. "Had nothing to do with it."

I got up to follow Hammett, who had headed for the door.

"Not you," Spainy said. "Got a few more questions for you. We're going to trade recipes for rabbit stew."

Stanford was fast disappearing and the good old boy was almost back.

"Mr. Peters and I are together," Hammett said.

"Just a question or two," Spainy said, holding his ham hands up to show they were empty and he was honest.

"I'll be fine," I said.

Spainy beamed love, good will and underlying hostility worthy of Billy Sunday.

"I'll wait outside," Hammett said.

"Have a cup of Postum before you go," said Spainy, as J.V., hair falling over her eyes, balanced her way through the door with a cup of hot liquid.

"No, thanks," said Hammett and went through the door as J.V. put the hot cup on the table in front of the Chief. J.V. wiped her palms on her uniform and smiled tentatively, like a mother who had baked a special treat for her spoiled child. The Chief eyed the brew and J.V. with distaste.

"It'll do," he said.

J.V. looked at me and backed out of the room, closing the door behind her.

"Good girl," Spainy said, picking up the cup. "A bit obsequious."

"Good word," I said.

"Damn good word," Spainy said, drinking and making a face. He put the cup down and added, "Can't believe this stuff is good for you. Want to know another good word? *Lepus*. Means rabbits."

I had a couple of good comments but I managed to keep from letting them spurt out.

"You want to tell me what's going on?" he said.

Behind his back, through the window looking out on the street, I could see the traffic roll slowly by. Angel Springs wasn't in a hurry. Neither was Chief Spainy.

"There's a war going on," I said. "Russian front is shaky. Rommel is backing up in North Africa. Port Moresby looks like it might fall in the Pacific."

"You a joker?" asked Spainy, pointing his cup at me.

"No," I said, straight-faced.

On the street behind his back, I saw Hammett come out of the station, shade his eyes and look toward the sun. He plunged his hands into his pockets, looked back at the station and stepped to the sidewalk to pace and wait.

"You're a talker," he said. "That's good. I'm a listener. Now you just tell me what you know and I'll listen."

A car pulled up in front of Hammett on the street, a DeSoto. I sat up to be sure. It was Wylie and Conrad.

"I'm listening and I don't hear anything," Spainy said. "I got some time."

"On the street," I said, pointing, as Wylie and Conrad, still in overalls, got out of the car. Hammett stood his ground. Wylie shielded something with his body. I figured it was a gun because Hammett looked up at Spainy's window, gave a lop-sided grin followed by a thin-shouldered shrug, and got into the car.

"They're out there," I said still pointing. "They're kidnapping Hammett."

Spainy lifted his eyebrows but he didn't turn.

"That a fact? Right in front of police headquarters," he said, sipping again at his Postum. "Who's kidnapping him?"

"The two guys at Pudge . . . Block's house," I said. "Look, for God's sake."

Conrad was in the back seat. Wylie was in front with Hammett at his side.

"The guys . . ." Chief Spainy said, nodding. "I thought there were no guys."

"There were. We just said that because . . . things were getting too complicated," I explained. "Will you take a look?"

I got out of the chair, and started to move around the desk to show him as the DeSoto began to pull away from the curb. Spainy came out of the chair and kicked it behind him. It rolled back against the wall as he stepped in front of me. He still hadn't looked out the window and I was beginning to understand whose pocket he was in.

"Sit back down," Spainy said, fists balled.

"Do something, Spainy," I said as the DeSoto pulled away and turned the nearest corner.

"Don't ask for the dance if you don't know the steps," said Spainy.

"They're gone," I said, teeth clenched, looking into his eyes. "They're gone, you damn pachyderm."

One ham-handed fist came up and caught me in the stomach, doubling me over. The other hand, an uppercut, caught me on the left ear. I had a good shot at his groin. I didn't take it. I staggered back to the chair at a ninety-degree angle.

"I'm the one with the big words around here," he said, jabbing his thumb at his chest. "You are more than fifty miles from home and in a lonely place. Hammett's got some friends, but you . . ."

"Friends like Pintacki?" I asked.

"None of your damn business, rabbit," said Spainy, still standing.

My ear was bleeding, but I wouldn't give him the satisfaction of seeing me touch it.

"A couple of guys I think work for Pintacki just kidnapped Dashiell Hammett from in front of your building," I said, holding back the pain in my stomach. The ear didn't really hurt. It just throbbed and demanded attention I wasn't giving it. "He's a real famous man, Spainy. Something happens to him and you'll be riding herd on your rabbits full time."

"Got no time for this, Peters. I warn you." The first tremor of nervousness appeared in his voice. "You got some answers for me?"

"None," I said, sitting up as straight as I could. "I've got other things I'd like to give you but I think I'll save them for the holidays."

Spainy laughed, a false laugh that shook his chest and turned his face red.

"Threats," he said, between bellows. "God, rabbit, you got a nerve. I give you that. I pick you up by the ears and you're still ready to bite. I'll give you that."

"You didn't give it to me," I said. "I earned it. How about I leave now or you throw me back in the cell and waste more taxpayer money? If I'm not out of here soon, I'd guess Hammett will call his friend Pintacki."

"Thought old Hammett had been kidnapped?"

"Pick your story," I said softly.

"I'll pick your . . . get the hell out of here. I got reports, a lunch talk at the Kiwanis in Overton. Get the hell out."

I stood up, ready to give him a Jimmy Cagney smile, but he was rummaging through his desk for something or nothing. I ignored the pain in my stomach, walked reasonably straight to the door and went out. My hand went to my ear and came down bloody. I leaned against the wall, felt my tender gut and looked around for a washroom or a water fountain. I saw J.V. looking up at me from her desk a few feet away. She was talking on the telephone again but not looking through me. The look on her face was full of sympathy. Another blue-uniformed woman, in her sixties, was standing near J.V.'s desk looking at a clipboard and tapping her toes to a Kay Kyser song on the radio.

I spotted a drinking fountain a few feet away and moved to it to moisten my hand and put it to my ear.

The place wasn't bustling with life. I found a semiclean hand-kerchief in my pocket and turned it wet, cold and red in seconds.

"I've got some stuff in my desk," came a voice behind me. I turned to face J.V. Her skin was clear and tan and her eyes concerned, a good combination.

"He might come out," I said, looking at Chief Spainy's door.

"God," she said, clasping her hands. "Wait. I'm on lunch break. Come on."

She motioned for me to follow her, swept her dark hair away from her face and headed for the exit, glancing back at Chief Spainy's door.

"Be back at one, Dorothy," J.V. said to the toe-tapper in uniform.

Dorothy, short, gray and distracted, nodded and kept on tapping and reading as we went out the front door.

"This way," J.V. said, walking a foot in front of me, probably to avoid the drip of my bleeding ear. "It's not far."

And it wasn't. We crossed the broad central street of Angel Springs, passed the hardware store and a pair of high-fashion women's clothing shops, went around the corner past a Rexall Drugstore and into a doorway between the Paris Golf Shop and Sharon's Luncheonette.

"Up here," she said, and up the narrow wooden stairway we went to two doors above the shops. She brushed her dark falling hair away again, pulled a small ring of keys from her pocket and opened the door on the right.

"Just a second," she said, indicating I should wait.

I waited and she went in. I could hear her shoes clopping quickly inside, and through the open door I could see the bedroom—living room and part of a kitchen. She was back in a few seconds, handing me a towel which I placed over my tender ear.

"Come in," she said, backing inside and wiping her palms on her hips.

I went in. The room wasn't quite a mess, but the bed hadn't been made and the morning newspaper and a few magazines were scattered on the floor. Beyond, in the small kitchen, I could see a few dishes on the table. Back in the living-bedroom there was a combination radio and record player in a corner near the windows.

Records were stacked on the floor and on a small white table. Still holding the towel to my ear, I walked to the window and looked out onto one of Angel Spring's business streets.

"It's a mess. I know," J.V. said, looking around the room.

I gave her a lop-sided smile and looked at the framed posters on her wall. They were all old and yellowing, and all were for operas.

"I like opera," she said, almost apologetically. "Sad ones especially. Listen every Saturday to the Met, even have Deems Taylor's book here someplace." She glanced around in vain search for the book.

"That's my favorite," she said, looking up at a poster for *Tosca* which featured a man in a white wig clasping the wrists of a woman who kneeled in obvious pain before him. "He's torturing her boyfriend in the other room," she said, taking a step toward me. "He wants her to . . . you know, but she kills the bad guy at the end of the second act. Third act she tries to free her boyfriend but he gets shot and she jumps off a tower."

"Sad," I said, taking the towel from my ear. The bleeding wasn't too bad.

"You're telling me," she said. "The music is beautiful. You want to hear it?"

"Someone kidnapped my friend," I said. "I saw it through the Chief's window. Two men in overalls named Wylie and Conrad. You know them?"

J.V. had moved to the record player and was fingering through her records.

"I don't know," she said nervously, then she turned to me. "Maybe we better just skip the opera. I'll bandage your ear and you can go . . ."

"You've heard of them," I said gently. "They work for Pintacki, don't they?"

"God. What have I done?" J.V. said, looking at me. "My mother, my father, my sister Bernice and my brother David-Arnold said I've got stray cat-itis and it was going to get me in trouble some day. God, don't make this the day. I'm not ready for it."

"They have my friend," I said, moving past her and aiming for the bathroom.

"The Chief . . ." she started, her voice cracking slightly.

". . . wouldn't believe me. This Pintacki has him under his thumb," I said from the small, cluttered bathroom. There was hair on the soap. Used towels hung from shower racks, towel racks, and over the top of the toilet. I used the bloody towel to wash my ear and then checked myself in the mirror. The thin scratch from the cat was almost gone. The ear was red and stuck out a little more than usual but it would be all right with a piece of tape. I found one in the medicine cabinet behind the Dr. Lyon's tooth powder.

The bathroom smelled slightly of sweat and soap and reminded me of something, somewhere, and someone.

"Give me a hand with this tape," I said, coming out of the bathroom.

J.V. was standing nervously near the record player. A stack of records rested on the spindle over the turntable. One of them dropped, bristled, crackled and came on. A woman sang in anguish and Italian through the cheap speaker.

J.V. sighed and moved toward me. Her breasts moved softly under the blue blouse and she smelled slightly of the washroom I'd just come out of. She avoided my eyes and taped my ear with shaking fingers.

"Beautiful," I said.

She stepped back away from my touch.

"The music," I explained, pointing at the record player.

"Right," she agreed.

"And you, too," I added. "Thanks for helping me."

"Stray cat-itis," she said. "You hungry?"

"Yes," I said.

The woman on the record sang out in Italian. J.V. turned her back and moved into the kitchen. I followed her.

"Sandwiches," she said, moving to the refrigerator. "Liver sausage, or I could do some bacon fast." She looked up at a clock on the wall above her small sink. The clock was embedded in a red enameled outline of a windmill. "I've got about forty minutes."

The kitchen was small. I stood next to her as she worked.

"Pintacki," I repeated. "How do I get to his place?"

"It's hard to find," J.V. said without looking at me.

"Show me," I said.

"Got to get back to work," she said. "Beer?"

"I saw a Dad's root beer in the refrigerator," I said. "I'll have that and directions on a map."

"I don't think the Chief would like it if I . . ." she said as she generously swabbed a slice of bread with Miracle Whip.

"I don't think he would either," I said, opening the refrigerator and pulling out the Dad's. "But that doesn't mean it would be wrong to do it."

"I don't know," she said, putting two liver-sausage sandwiches on a plate and licking the Miracle Whip from her fingers. If she hadn't done that, I could have kept my distance, but she was close and smelled of sweat and looked like someone who needed. I touched her arm. She turned suddenly to face me, slightly frightened.

"I'm not going to hurt you," I said, holding my hands up. "If you want me to, I'll take my sandwich and go. I just thought . . ."

The look of fear didn't leave her. She stepped in front of me, her big brown eyes scanning my face for something. I reached over and pushed a strand of hair from her face and she came to me, her breasts against my sore chest, her mouth against mine, and open and warm and tasting of Miracle Whip.

The kiss was long and soft. Her arms were around my neck, touching my hair. I was the one who pulled back to catch my breath. The woman behind us sang as I looked into J.V.'s eyes.

"I've never done anything like this. Not ever," she said. "It's crazy."

"You mean you're a . . . you've never," I said.

"No," she said with a slight smile, inches from my face. "I was married for a few years when I was twenty. His name was Alfred. He just left one day and never came back. I never got a divorce. It's been . . . I don't know . . . about ten years since I . . ."

I kissed her. Her face was soft and warm.

"You sure you want me?" she said, pulling her head back to seek my eyes. "I don't think I'm any good at this kind of thing. God. Listen to me. What are we talking about here? I must be going nuts. I just met you. I don't know anything about you."

I kissed her again and she sighed. "What the hell?" she said, taking my hand and leading me back into the living room. "How long will this take?"

"I don't know," I said.

"I've got to be back at the station in thirty-five minutes or the Chief will come looking for me," she said as we sat on the unmade bed.

I unbuttoned her uniform, brushed back her hair and looked at her breasts. They were round, pinkish-white and beautiful. I'd never made love to a cop before. She reached over with trembling fingers and unbuttoned my shirt.

"The Chief would come himself if you didn't come back on time?" I asked.

"He's my brother," she said.

"Of course," I said.

The woman sang on in Italian, and was joined by a man with a deep voice. J.V. and I rolled and wrapped under the rough blue blanket. She was deep, warm, moist and strong, and she hummed contentedly. I didn't feel too bad myself. The record ended. The spindle was empty. The automatic arm lifted and clicked itself off.

"Time," she whispered in my ear.

"Don't know," I said. "My watch is never right."

She kissed me and rolled over to stand up. There was plenty of her but she wasn't fat. Ample, plump.

"Men stay away from me in Angel Springs," she called, moving to check the clock in the kitchen and returning with the two sandwiches and a glass of semiflat Dad's root beer for me. "My brother . . . you know."

"Sort of," I said, accepting the liver sausage. "You were great."

"Thanks," she said with a blush and smile, a cheekful of sandwich. "God, you don't think I'll have a baby? I mean, just from one time?"

"I don't think so," I said.

She looked at the window, at her sandwich, at me.

"I don't think so, either," she repeated without great confidence. "No offense, but do people your age . . . I mean I looked at the sheet on you . . . can you . . . do you have babies?"

"We cling to life," I said, sitting up gingerly. My chest was covered with gray and black hair. We both looked at it and at the discolored circle where J.V.'s brother had hit me. "It's always possible some ancient sperm of mine could dig down deep for a final hallelu."

"I think I'm okay anyway," she said, finishing off her sandwich and reaching for her panties at the foot of the bed. "I got seven minutes."

I reached out and grasped her wrist. She looked scared again. I pulled her hand to my mouth, kissed her finger—tasting liver sausage this time—and then let her go.

"God," she said with a sigh. "I love operas, the Italian ones; the women fall in love right away, sing beautiful songs, do dumb things and kill themselves. They sing pretty but they are dumb. I don't sing and I hope I'm not dumb, but I'll show you how to get to Pintacki's place."

While I sat up in her bed, eating my sandwich and looking across at the scowling face of a man with a sword on a poster of *Il Trovatore,* J.V. finished dressing and came back with a map of the area—Angel Springs, Palm Springs and a few oasis stops. She showed me the roads leading into the desert, and indicated with a small penciled *X* about where I'd find Pintacki's. Before she could stand up, I touched her cheek and kissed her. She closed her eyes, kissed back and then pulled away.

"You'll see me before you go?" she said, adjusting her belt. "I mean before you leave Angel Springs?"

"Promise," I said. "J.V.? What's your name?"

"Jean," she said. "The V doesn't mean anything."

"Jean," I said. "How would you like a real stray cat? I really have one."

She had moved to the door by now and paused to look at my face to see if I was joking. She could see I wasn't.

"I . . . maybe," she said. "I'll think about it."

And she was gone.

I finished my Dad's, put on my pants and found J.V.'s phone in the corner near the record player. I called Shelly at the office, asked for messages, and said there was a chance his new patient might not make his appointment tomorrow morning.

"Where's my patient?" he said angrily when he heard that last revelation. "Where is he?"

"He's been kidnapped, Shel," I said.

"What?" Shelly bleated. "You took him somewhere. I want him back. He said he'd pay cash."

"I appreciate your humanity and concern, Sheldon," I said, "but he's been kidnapped. As soon as I get him back, you can finish mutilating him."

"It's not right, Toby, to do that," he said.

"I apologize, Sheldon," I said. "Has anyone been looking for me?"

"Not right," Shelly repeated.

"Anyone looking for me?" I shouted.

"Yes," he shouted back. "Some soldier. I'll get the note."

A pause while Shelly rummaged around and finally found it.

"Major Castle. Left a message. Wants a report. Left a number. You want it?"

I wanted it. Shelly gave it to me and I assured him once again that I'd deliver Hammett unto him in at least one piece.

When I finally got rid of Shelly, who insisted on telling me about his plan to hire a dental assistant named Louise-Mary, I called the number Major Castle had left. A voice came on, a voice I didn't recognize. It was a man, but I couldn't tell what age.

"Major Castle," I said. "Tell him it's Toby Peters."

"He's not here," said the man. "He will be calling in at fourteen hundred hours."

"Tell him I'm in Angel Springs," I said. "And I may be near Lansing. If . . ."

And then the voice of General MacArthur broke in.

"Peters," he said. "We must return to the Pacific by the day after tomorrow. This continent is in imminent danger. A Japanese submarine has shelled the coast of Oregon at Fort Stevens. A Japanese airplane dropped incendiary bombs on the southern coast of Oregon. Defense plants along the coast are being hurriedly protected by barrage balloons and antiaircraft batteries. This Lansing affair, this distraction from my primary task, must be resolved before I return to the theater of battle."

"I'll do what I can, General," I said.

"I can accept nothing less than success," MacArthur replied. "I can live with temporary setbacks, but I do not accept them."

"I'll call when I have anything," I said.

And the General was off the line.

The man who had answered the phone came back on the line to say, "This number may not exist beyond this call. How can Major Castle reach you?"

"Leave messages at my office."

I hung up before he could come up with anything else, put my dishes in the sink, dressed, and left a note for J.V. along with two dollars to pay for the phone calls. I was on the street in a few minutes and found a cab around the corner in front of the Rexall. Fifteen minutes later I was behind the wheel of my Crosley in Pudge's driveway. Another car was blocking my way, a big blue Buick Eight convertible with a grill that looked like steel teeth. I had enough room to turn, drive over the lawn and bounce onto the street. The door to Pudge's house opened and an angry blond woman in white stepped out to glare at me. I figured it was the grieving Widow Pudge.

I stopped the car and got out. The angry look on her face turned to fear and she backed up.

"Mrs. Block?" I asked.

"What do you want?" she said, ready to slam the door on me.

She was hard, pretty, thin and tan, not my type at all but the best money could buy at her age.

"My cat," I said.

"Your . . ." she began, and the cat, big and orange, dashed through her legs and ran over to rub itself against my leg. I picked him up and felt him purr against me through my Windbreaker. It was a sunny day and I was feeling warm and ready with the memory of J.V. still in my mouth.

". . . cat," I finished and headed for my car.

"You've torn up my lawn," she screamed, gaining courage now that the mashed-nose intruder was heading away.

"Pudge's insurance will cover it," I said. "Enjoy yourself."

I got in the car, put the cat down in the back seat, checked the map J.V. had given me, made sure my .38 was still in the glove compartment, and headed for the desert.

7

The desert wasn't far. Angel Springs was a green island on the edge of a sea of sand, sagebrush, cactus and distant hills. Just after I lost sight of town I stopped at a small truck stop called Marty and Matty's. Marty and Matty's had been announced by weathered roadside signs promising good food, cheap gas and hospitality.

Marty and Matty weren't doing much business. I pulled up next to one of the two Sinclair pumps and waited. No one came. I beeped the Crosley's tin horn. The cat screeched and jumped into my lap. Finally, a lanky woman in a baseball cap and overalls came out of the station-restaurant, an oily rag in her hands, and cowboyed toward me. I got out of the car, closing the cat inside.

"Gas?" the woman asked. She was weathered down, and her black and gray hair suggested she wasn't young but might not yet be old.

"Gas," I said. "A pair of Pepsi's, a couple of sandwiches, one for here and one to go, something for my cat and some information."

"Gas first," said the woman, moving to the pump.

I moved past the pumps into the station, where I found a short-order counter with four stools. There were two tables in the small space beyond the counter, each with three chairs. The tables were wood and everything was covered with a thin layer of sand. A large painting of a snow-covered valley filled one wall. It was covered with sand too.

I took a seat on one of the stools after wiping off the dust and picked up a sandy copy of last week's *American Weekly*. I flipped pages till the woman came back through the screen door.

"Eighty cents for the gas," she said. "What kind of sandwiches you want?"

"What kind you got?"

"Cheese," she said.

"Sounds good," I said.

She moved behind the counter, washed her hands in the sink with a bar of Lava.

"You Marty or Matty?" I asked.

"Neither," she said. "Marty's my husband. Matty's my son. Marty's in England someplace, in the army. Matty's in Seattle, navy. Cat eat cheese?"

"Don't know," I said.

"Let's give him a can of chicken noodle soup," she said. "Give it to him warm without adding the water."

"Sounds good," I said, watching her open a bag of bread and pull out a couple of slices.

"You said you wanted information?"

"Man called Pintacki," I said. "Lives out this way someplace."

The woman paused and looked at me, slice of cheese in one hand, butter knife in the other.

"You a friend or kin of his?" she asked.

"Neither," I said. "I've never met him. We've got business."

She went on making the sandwich.

"Suit yourself," she said. "But don't trust him."

"He has two men working for him, Wylie and Conrad," I went on.

"You asking or telling?" she said, plopping the sandwich in front of me on a small plate, along with a bag of Fritos.

"Asking," I said, reaching for the bag while she kneeled and came up with a can of Campbell's chicken noodle.

"He's got two men working for him, Wylie and Conrad," the woman said. She opened the refrigerator, came up with a Pepsi, opened it and put it on the counter next to me. "You want a glass?"

"No," I said.

"Good," she said, taking off her baseball cap and wiping her brow with the sleeve of her rolled-up shirt. "Shouldn't leave animals in the car out here, even with the windows open. You want me to get your cat?"

"Sure," I said, washing down a dry bit of sandwich with Pepsi.

"I'll feed him," she said, opening the can of soup and pouring it into a metal bowl. "Okay?"

"Okay," I said. "Conrad and Wylie drive a DeSoto. You happen to see them drive by this morning?"

"Coming or going?"

"Either one," I said.

"Both," she said. "Stopped for gas on the way to town. Shot by about two hours back without slowing down."

"See anyone in the car with them?"

"Didn't notice," she said.

I swiveled on the squeaky stool and watched her move out of the station and over to the Crosley. She opened the door and scooped the cat out. She ran her rough hand over his back and placed the bowl on the ground next to the pump. I finished the sandwich, Fritos, and the rest of the Pepsi. The cat finished eating. The woman put him under one arm, picked up the bowl in her free hand and came back inside.

"Good animal," she said, dropping him on the counter in front of me.

"Thanks," I said. "How'd you like to adopt him?"

"Can't," she said, dropping the empty bowl in the sink behind the counter. "Got a dog, Harold. He's running out somewhere but he'd eat your cat in two minutes. Harold's a good dog, but he figures the station and the twenty miles around it is his territory."

"Pintacki," I reminded her.

"He and Harold got similar ideas, only Pintacki's are a bit grander and less realistic," she said.

"You mean . . ." I said.

"I don't mean anything," she said, making a second cheese sandwich for the road. "You want to ask him? You go about ten miles farther east down the road. You'll see a wire fence on the right. Keep going till you hit a gate. No name on it. That's where you want. No more information. Harold and I got to live out here and I want no trouble till my men get back."

"And then?" I asked as she handed me a bottle of Pepsi and the wrapped sandwich. The cat played with a leftover Frito.

"Maybe they'll have a talk with Pintacki," she said.

"Thanks," I said. "What's the damage?"

"Buck five," she said. "That covers the two cents on the bottle and the bottle opener in the bag. Information's free. So's the advice. Turn around and go back to town."

She flipped on the radio and a transcription of "Treasury Star Parade" came on. Fredric March shouted "millions for defense" and a chorus sang "Any Bonds Today." I fished a dollar and a quarter out of my pocket, laid it on the counter and picked up the cat. "Thanks," I said.

"You got what you paid for," she said, pocketing the money instead of putting it in the cash register.

I took the cat to the car, got in, started the car and turned on the radio as I pulled out of the station and headed down the road. Someone on the radio said, "MacArthur can't win this war alone," and a chorus of voices agreed to pitch in and help him. Then they talked about making room to house families who might have to be evacuated from the East Coast in case of a German attack. The cat and I were depressed. I turned off the radio and he purred.

The desert moved by, brush cactus, patches of wild plants and no sign of any houses or human life. A lizard skittered across the road. I managed to miss him. About three minutes later a Plymouth coupe headed toward me, going in the direction of Angel Springs. I caught a flash of a fat man in a white tee shirt as the car zipped past, and watched him disappear in my rearview mirror.

"Cat," I said, looking at the flat, dry, seemingly endless desert. "This might not be a good idea."

The cat had curled up in the passenger seat for an after-lunch nap. He didn't answer. I found the barbed-wire fence and followed it for about two miles. No Trespassing signs stood erect every half mile or so. I drove till I hit the gate, the gate the woman at the truck stop had told me about. I didn't stop. I kept going for another mile or so past more No Trespassing signs till I came to the corner of the wire fence and hit open desert. I pulled off the road and drove behind a clump of yucca trees.

I got out of the car and walked to the road. The Crosley was small and reasonably well hidden behind the yuccas. Not perfect, but it would have to do. I went back to the car, opened the windows a little more, petted the cat and, with a thin trickle of sweat finding its way between the gray hairs on my chest, I leaned back and fell asleep.

A few seconds later the car was surrounded by Japanese soldiers. They came out of holes in the sand, from behind a stray cactus, from the branches of the nearby yuccas. They wore blue uniforms and were led by Chief Spainy. I tried to start the car. It wouldn't start. Bayonets were shining in the sun.

"His ear, boys," Spainy shouted. "Get his ear. J.V. wants his damn ear."

I fumbled for my .38, found it. It drooped in my hand. I tried to pull it together, get the barrel to straighten up so I could shoot it, but it lay like melting licorice. When the first Japanese soldier was about to skewer me through the open window I woke up with a shudder.

It was almost dark. A car whined past on the road, heading into the desert. I shivered and looked down at the cat pushing its nose into the paper bag.

"I'll give you a hand," I said, after I closed the windows.

I tore the sandwich in two, put my half on my lap and tore the cat's half into little pieces. I placed the pieces on the flattened bag and he dug into it, waving his tail. I downed my sandwich in two bites.

"I'm stalling, cat," I said.

The cat cleaned his paws with his pink tongue and ignored me.

"Let's go."

I got out and let the cat follow me. He stuck his nose in the air, twitched and shuddered. I pulled my flashlight, my jack and an old sweater out of the small trunk. The sweater was dirty and I'd meant to have it cleaned weeks ago. I locked the car and hid the key under a rock near one of the yuccas. I put the sweater on under the Windbreaker, looked around and moved to the fence. The cat jumped over the lowest strand of wire. I moved to the closest post and set up the jack where wire met post.

The cat sat watching me and waiting. The jack slipped in the sand a few times, then caught and with each clack lifted the lower stand. When it was high enough, I slithered under the wire and joined the cat.

"Well," I told the cat, "this is the way out. Think you can remember it?"

The cat thought the question was beneath him. He turned away from me, looking at something I didn't see, and started to move slowly away from the fence. What the hell? I followed him. I didn't want to turn on the flashlight unless I had to. It bounced inside the pocket of my Windbreaker, balancing the weight of the .38 in the other pocket.

It was dark about twenty minutes after we started, but the moon was high and almost full and the stars were clear, millions of stars, stars you never see in the city. Once in a while when I was a kid my old man used to take my brother and me out to the desert on Sunday to look at the cactus and wait for the night. My father, a grocer by trade, a dreamer by inclination, would sit with us on the hood of our Ford with blankets wrapped around us. We'd look up at the sky, eat sandwiches he'd made in the grocery and say nothing. Even though he was older, Phil always got bored first. If he was in a good mood, he'd poke me in the ribs and climb back in the car. If he was in a bad mood, Phil would squeeze my arm hard enough to let me feel the grip of each finger for at least an hour. My father never said anything. I wondered if he had gone out to the desert with my mother before she died, but I never asked him.

"Cat, I think I see something."

The cat's eyes twinkled like stars as it turned to me.

"Cat, I don't think I like feeling this small. Between you and me, I'm not ready for it."

The cat meowed and padded across the sand and around something that scurried through the brush in front of us. The sand was solid in most places but we hit soft patches as we moved toward a glowing light ahead. My old man's watch said we'd walked about nine hours. I figured an hour was more like it.

The night stayed star-and-moon bright and the light in front of us got closer. About ten minutes later I could make out some of the shape of something in front of us against the sky. It looked big. Ten minutes farther and it looked even bigger.

"It's a goddam castle," I told the cat.

There were lights on. Not too many of them, but it looked like someone was awake. Smoke came from one of the turrets. When we were about five hundred yards away I could see the driveway and the road through the desert, probably to the main gate I had passed. In the driveway sat the DeSoto and a Willys station wagon.

The cat suddenly went wild. It meowed and turned away from the house.

"Shut up," I whispered. "Where the hell are you going?"

I looked at the house to see if someone had heard the meowing. Maybe they'd think it was a wild animal. Or maybe they'd come out to shoot whatever it was.

The cat dashed about thirty yards to the left and wailed. I ran, tripped and got to him. I was on my knees looking at the house and considering what the penalty might be for strangling a cat.

"You want to get us killed? You really think you have eight more lives?"

The cat went on howling and started clawing at the mound of sand it was perched on.

"All right," I said. "All right."

I clawed at the mound, not only to shut the cat up but because I didn't like the shape of the moonlit pile of sand. The cat was helping. I felt a piece of cloth first, then a finger and a hand. I scooped sand. The body wasn't buried very deep.

Even before I uncovered the face, I could tell it wasn't Hammett. The body was too young and the suit wasn't the one Hammett had on that morning. When I cleared the sand from the corpse's face I knew it was Andrew Lansing. He looked like a white clay version of the photograph I had, but there was no doubt it was him. I couldn't find a wound on the body so I turned it over. I was reasonably sure he didn't wander into the desert, cover himself like an Indian whose time had come, and simply die. The hole in the back of his skull said I was right. I turned him on his back again, dead eyes to the sky.

I checked his pockets. No money. No MacArthur report.

"Think you can find him again?" I asked the cat, softly picking him up.

He purred and I considered getting back to the car and going for help, not Spainy but the California State Police, but that would take hours and Hammett might also be under a mound by then if he wasn't already. I moved slowly toward the house, circling behind it where there was less light and less likelihood that someone might see me.

The house didn't just look like a small castle. It *was* a castle; stone, a pointed turret in each of the four corners, even oval barred windows and an oversized metal-reinforced wooden door.

"Don't get me killed, cat," I whispered, crouching as I moved slowly forward.

The cat licked the back of my hand. I pulled out my .38 and made my way to the rear of the castle in the desert. There was no cover. All I could do was move low and slowly, keeping an eye on the windows to see if anyone might be keeping an eye on the desert. My plan was to fall flat and lie quietly if I saw someone in the castle. Of course, there could have been someone in one of the darkened windows, someone I couldn't see. I did a Groucho walk for a dozen yards, dropped to my stomach and crept for another dozen yards, before I came nose-to-nose with a scorpion. The cat hissed. I got up, grabbed him and ran the last few yards to the castle.

Enough. The desert came right up to the house. I dropped the cat and reached for the wall. The rough stone was cool against my palm. I moved to the left, gun in hand, to a lighted window, and looked inside carefully. My shirt was sweat-drenched and sticky. I dried my palms on my pants.

There was no one in the room, a big library with floor-to-ceiling bookcases and a roaring fireplace.

"Cozy," I whispered to the cat and ducked under the window and moved around the corner to another lighted window. The cat followed, looking up at me curiously.

There was no one in this room, either; it was a big kitchen with a wooden worktable in the middle. Beyond the kitchen, at the side of the house, I found a door, heavy, solid. I pushed down on the iron handle expecting nothing and was surprised when it clicked open. The cat ran in ahead of me. I followed him, .38 in front of me. We were in a small alcove with a door in front of us. The alcove was lighted by a small overhead bulb that couldn't have been more than twenty-five watts. Through the wall to my left I could hear a machine, probably a generator, humming and grinding.

I pushed down on the handle of the second door and it opened into a dark room. The light from the alcove didn't help. I closed the door behind me slowly, and quietly, pulled out my flashlight, and turned the beam into the room. It fell on a face I recognized, the smiling craggy face of the trucker in Sheila's restaurant, the trucker who had saved Hammett and me from Conrad and Wylie. The cat was sitting in the trucker's lap.

Something clicked and the room was flooded with light. I blinked, and found myself facing not only the trucker in a chair but Wylie and Conrad standing next to him. Wylie held a shotgun. Conrad held a hunting rifle. The room seemed to be a servant's room, with a small table, chairs.

The trucker was wearing a blue shirt, a tie, and a white cardigan sweater.

"Took you almost forever to make your way here," the trucker said. "Conrad was for going out after you, but Conrad has not yet learned the virtue of patience. He may never learn."

I aimed my .38 at the trucker's chest.

"Pintacki," I said. "I want Hammett, now."

Pintacki smiled and stroked the traitor cat.

"Well, then, I'd better do what you say. You might shoot me. What do you say, men?"

He looked at Conrad and Wylie, whose guns were leveled at me. They didn't look back at him or answer.

"Got a feeling they don't want to make a deal," he said. "Got a feeling they knew you'd say something like that. I told them if you did to be ready to shoot you if you pulled the trigger. God almighty, Peters, you would make a hell of a mess. And all it would get you is killed. Wouldn't get you Hammett or the money or the papers. So, make your mind up. Shoot me and turn into an interesting pattern on the wall or put the gun down and have something to drink."

"I think I'll shoot," I said.

"Suit yourself," Pintacki said with a shrug. "Be a hell of a way to end all this. Problem is, I don't scare. I got things to do, and you don't get things done—important things—if you go through life scared. You've got to have nerve to give orders and get respect. Wylie and Conrad here know I mean it. They don't understand it but they know I mean it. I got things to do, Peters, so shoot or put the gun down. I'm ready to meet my maker if you are."

"I put the gun down and I wind up out in the desert like Lansing," I said. "I might as well take you with me."

"Like Lansing?" Pintacki said. "What the hell are you talking about? You know where Lansing is?"

"I know," I said. "So I've got nothing to lose here by taking you with me."

"What the hell are you jabbering about? I swear you are a confused creation of God," sighed Pintacki. "Lansing's hiding out somewhere. He gave me the papers and I let him keep the cash. That was our deal. I live up to my ideals and I abide by my deals. You can't expect loyalty if you don't live up to your word."

"You didn't kill Lansing?" I asked.

"I didn't kill Lansing if he is dead," Pintacki answered. "And if either of these two did so without telling me, they will eat every grain of the sand you walked through from now till Armageddon, which might not be that far away."

"We didn't kill Lansing," Wylie whined, looking even more like a bulldog.

"We didn't. I swear," Conrad chimed in.

"See?" said Pintacki with a smile.

"Hower," I said, feeling my grip on the gun loosen in my sweating and stiff fingers.

"Know about that one," Pintacki said. "Didn't kill him, though. Someone was trying to find Lansing and get to the papers before he got them to me. I think whoever it was asked Hower, who had the bad fortune not to know."

"Or maybe he did know," I said. "I knew."

"Don't know how you did that," said Pintacki. "That's one of the things we're going to talk about if you decide not to shoot me."

"You didn't kill anybody," I said. "You're a saint."

"A saint? No. A savior, maybe," he said. "I've not always been kind to people and I'll kill if it's the Lord's will, but the two sinners you mentioned, well, you'll have to take their bodies to another doorway. Listen, I've got a way out of this. I count five. When I hit it, you put down the gun, shoot, or Conrad and Wylie cut you down. Helps you with your decision. Fair enough?"

"I'm grateful," I said.

"One," said Pintacki, stroking the cat's chin.

I put my .38 on the table.

"Good choice," said Pintacki. "You can turn off your flashlight too."

I looked at the flashlight in my hand. I'd forgotten it was there. I turned it off, flexed my fingers, and waited.

"Hungry?" asked Pintacki. "Thirsty? How about a beer?"

I sat in the chair across from him.

"Conrad, put your gun down and get our guest a beer," Pintacki said. "Great cat."

"People seem to like him," I said. Conrad handed his gun to Wylie and moved toward the kitchen door. "You want to keep him? He seems to like you."

"Maybe," Pintacki said, looking at the cat. "I'll think on it."

"Hammett," I said. "Where is he?"

"In a room in the tower, just like a fairy tale. I gave him some books he wanted from the library and we had a good talk." Pintacki put the cat on the floor. "That man loves to read. Tells me he used to spend every day in the library in San Francisco. Walk his wife and child to the park, leave them there and spend the day reading, reading everything, anything. Can't say I care much for his lack of religion, or his politics, though. You a political man, Mr. Peters?"

Pintacki leaned forward on the table, his hands clasped as if my answer were the most important words he might ever hear.

"I don't think so," I said. "I voted for Willkie."

Pintacki shook his head.

"And you'd probably vote for MacArthur if he came back after the war," Pintacki said. "War hero comes home. Everyone loves him. Takes over the country. Sets us back twenty years. After this war, Peters, we won't have twenty years to make up. Look back at history. Jackson, Grant, Taylor. Military leaders set us back every time. Godless military leaders."

"I have a feeling you have a better idea," I said, as Conrad returned with open bottles of beer for all four of us on a tray, complete with pilsner glasses.

"I do have a better idea," Pintacki agreed, pushing a bottle of beer and a chilled glass toward me. "But we can wait till morning to discuss it."

We sat silently drinking our beer. Wylie drank his with his shotgun aimed at my head. The beer was cold and good. I grinned at Pintacki and he grinned back.

"It's late," he said, when we were finished. "I've got work to do and you've got thinking. Conrad and Wylie will show you to your room."

We went through the kitchen and then through a darkened, wood-paneled dining room. At the head of the table in the dining room was a huge thronelike chair. I had an idea of whose it might be.

Beyond the dining room was a hallway; marble floors, marble-topped tables, big ancient rugs on the walls. The cat followed me. Conrad and Wylie didn't have much to say. They guided me up the wooden staircase that wound around the wall of the hallway. We went down a corridor and through another door and up a narrow flight of worn-down stone stairs to a door, which Conrad moved ahead of me to open while Wylie stood below us, cradling his shotgun. The cat and I went in the room and the door was closed behind us.

I found the light switch and saw that I was in a small, round room with a bed. The walls were painted a dull gray and covered with oversized paintings of cowboy stars. Tom Mix, Ken Maynard, Buck Jones and Hoot Gibson smiled down at me. There was a table in the corner with a bedpan under it. The windows were narrow and barred.

"Cat," I said. "We've got a situation here."

The cat leaped onto the bed, curled up and fell asleep.

There was no radio in the room and nothing to read, not that I wanted to read, anyway. I ran my fingers along my stubbly cheek, sat down, took off my shoes, let the sand inside fall on the floor and then undressed down to my not-too-dirty undershorts. I flipped off the light.

It had been a tough night. It took me ten whole minutes to fall asleep.

8

A door closing, a big, thick familiar door covered with something soft and sticky, maybe honey, closed in front of me. I had to open it. Something was behind me but I didn't want to touch the door. Light exploded over my shoulder. I winced, opened my eyes and knew I'd been dreaming. Conrad stood near the barred window, his hand still on the drapes he had opened to let in the morning. The window was open and a slab of warm air eased through it.

"I dreamt I was in Cincinnati," I said, tasting tin in my mouth.

Conrad didn't answer. He turned, folded his arms over the front of his overalls and faced me, letting me see that he was wearing a holster in which rested a large pistol.

"How are you this morning, Conrad?" I asked, sitting up and rubbing my palm over my bristly face.

"I had my way I'd punch your face in," Conrad said.

"Yeah," I said, looking around the room. "It is one of those days that makes you glad to be alive."

"Punch it right in," Conrad repeated seriously. His eyes went dreamy, as if he were imagining my face being crushed by his fist. It gave him a calm, almost benevolent look.

The cat purred out from under the bed, stretched, blinked and looked around.

"I think you have something to clean up under the bed, Conrad," I said.

"I don't like cats," he said. "I'd snap their necks if I had my way."

"Then," I said, standing up and moving on not-yet-steady legs to the dresser against the wall, over which hung a mirror and on which sat a round, solid-amber ashtray, which immediately gave me ideas—"the cats of the world and I are grateful that you don't have your way and, judging from your need for supervision, probably never will have your way."

"I'd snap your neck too," he said.

"Don't doubt it for a minute, my friend. Jesus. Look at that."

I pointed at my face in the mirror. The dark hair flecked with gray clumped in different directions. The threatening beard was solid gray. It was depressing. The face itself had seen better days. It had to have seen better days.

"What more could you do to a face like that, Conrad? I ask you. No, I think you should stick with visions of neck-snapping. Smashing my face wouldn't give you much satisfaction."

I grinned at Conrad, who unfolded his arms, understanding for the first time that he was being needled.

"I don't like jokes," he said.

"No one likes what they don't understand," I said.

Conrad stepped toward me, his mouth slightly opened, his teeth clenched.

"I think you're making jokes some more," he said.

Conrad was ready to be plucked. He was bigger, younger, confident, and he had the gun. Nothing to worry about. Tired old detective with a gray beard. He'd crack me with his bare hands like a coconut. The cat could tell something was going on. He jumped up on the bed, sat and, pretending to be half asleep, moved his eyes from me to Conrad lumbering toward me.

I backed away from him and put my hand on the dresser. My fingers touched the heavy amber ashtray.

"Remember, Conrad," I reminded him. "You don't have your way."

"I can just squeeze a little and make your eyes pop," he said, holding his hands in front of me to show me what he planned to squeeze with.

If luck were with me—and it owed me one—and Conrad's head were made of anything less than the chrome steel that failed to keep King Kong in check, he would be dreaming of Cincinnati in a few seconds and I would be out looking for Hammett with Conrad's gun in my hand.

I blocked his view of the ashtray with my body and got a firm grip on the rough amber while I held up my free hand as if to keep Conrad back.

"I guess I can't tell you I was just joking," I said. "You wouldn't know what I was talking about."

He was in front of me now, ready. I was ready too, but the door opened and Wylie stepped in, shotgun in hand. He looked at the mirror and I could tell that he saw my hand on the ashtray.

"Conrad," he said. "The man's about to spread what little brains you got around the room. Just step away from him. Mr. P's waiting."

"If I had my way . . ." Conrad whispered to me.

"You'd never grow old," I finished.

"You are a genuine crazy," Conrad said.

"Come on," Wylie said. "Let's get him cleaned up. Show's at 0900 hours."

"Cat pooed under the bed," Conrad said.

"Pooed? You mean he shit? Well, clean it up and come down," said Wylie with a sigh.

Conrad stayed behind and Wylie headed me and the cat down the stairs to the lower landing and into a large bathroom with a claw-foot tub. On a rack hung a blue knit short-sleeve pullover shirt. My shoes stood on the floor with a pair of fresh socks rolled neatly between them.

"Shave with the Gem razor on the sink and wash up. New toothbrush and powder right there. Even got a comb and aftershave. Mr. P likes guests to be clean and respectable for the show."

Wylie stayed safely away from me while I shaved, washed, brushed, put on the shirt, socks and my shoes. The cat leaped onto the sink and licked a few splashes of water from the counter.

"Now?" I asked.

"Show time," said Wylie, pointing me out the bathroom door. We made our way down the stairs and through the front hall, where the desert light through the windows turned the inside of the castle orange. We made a turn into the big dining room, and Wylie nodded me to a seat across from Dashiell Hammett. The vacant place was set with plate, utensils, cup, glass of orange juice and linen napkin. I sat.

Hammett was shaven, wearing a white shirt and tie and an amused look. Pintacki sat at the head of the table, between us and not too close, a six-shooter on the table within easy reach. Next to the six-shooter was a movie projector.

Pintacki, open collar, looking cool in spite of the desert heat, motioned to Wylie, who walked over and handed Pintacki his shotgun. Then Wylie disappeared through the door to the kitchen.

"Mr. Hammett and I have been discussing what I should do with you both," said Pintacki, slicing a piece of ham and putting it in his mouth. "I'm for making you my guests for an indefinite period, till I sort out a few things. He's for getting you both killed. Now, that might be what I'll decide to do anyway but I thought you might like to have a little hope. A little hope can't hurt. Might help."

"I'm with you," I said to Pintacki as Wylie came back through the door with a plate of food and moved along the table to hand it to me. When he had, Wylie backed away, retrieved his shotgun and went to stand in the corner.

"Mr. Pintacki wants to be king of the United States," said Hammett. "I think a king should be decisive."

"King?" I asked, digging into my plate of scrambled eggs, ham and potatoes.

"Not quite," said Pintacki with a smile. "I have plans for this country. Douglas MacArthur is an ambitious man. With the information supplied to me by Andrew Lansing, I may well convince the General to implement some of my major ideas when he becomes President. If not, I may give the information to a rival, who would be very grateful. The situation in this country is grave. The military has controlled our destiny. It's time we controlled the military." Pintacki leaned across the table and whispered, "Frankly, Peters, I am very wealthy. But it don't mean a doodle and a fart if I can't do something with it, like save the goddam country, if you know what I mean."

"Makes sense to me," I said.

"And to me," Hammett agreed.

"You're humoring me, gentlemen," said Pintacki with a laugh, as he dabbed his lips with a linen napkin. "I'm used to that, but I am a determined man. I didn't want any of this to happen. The world is a mound of trash and tribulation. Anyone with half a mind and a sense of smell knows it. I built this place to get away. Got a five-year supply of water, a generator with two backups, fuel for the rest of my natural or unnatural life, whichever comes first, and no telephone. Let the whole damn world bomb itself to pieces. I didn't give a lizard's ass and tail. But I thought about it. I sat here night after night watching the classics of the cinema and I thought about it. Finally decided I'd give the United States one more chance."

"Decent of you," I said.

"Maybe so," said Pintacki. "I like to think God found me like a saint in the desert and singled me out. Want some coffee?"

"Yeah," I said.

Wylie ambled into the kitchen.

"Where was I?" Pintacki said, looking at Hammett and me.

"God found you," I said.

"Right," said Pintacki, playing with a piece of slightly burned and probably cold toast. "Paper today has an article by some kid named Walter Cronkite about the Japs blowing up the *Wakefield*. Just a transport, you say, but it's not. It's a damn symbol. It took me years to understand that you can't run from reality. You can't run from symbols. You can build a castle in the desert but they'll come and find you, the way you two did, come and find you and ask you to pay taxes, fill out papers, give money to people you don't like."

I considered reminding Pintacki that he had some responsibility for our being there.

"So," Pintacki said after an enormous sigh, "I figured if I couldn't be left alone by the country, and God was calling me anyway, I'd have to come out of the desert like Moses, like the saints, and take charge. You following this so far?"

Wylie put his shotgun down and walked down to us with pot of coffee. He poured some for me and Hammett.

"We are fascinated," said Hammett.

"Maybe so, maybe no," said Pintacki. "Lost my boy in the first days of this war. Not asking for sympathy. Don't want it. I lost a boy and that's that. If I'd have got the word sooner, I might have done something to save him, but that's the past and past is past and he is in God's domain."

Wylie placed the coffee pot out of our reach and returned to his corner.

"Sorry," I said.

"'Bout what?" asked Pintacki.

"Your son," I said.

"House boy," Pintacki shouted. "Not my son. Filipino house boy. Blew him to pieces on some island. Can't get help anymore. Not out this far."

"I think you should shoot us or let us go," said Hammett. "I don't think I want to listen to any more of this."

Pintacki's face went red and he dropped his napkin on his plate.

"I'm still fascinated," I said.

"I have a plan, a platform, an agenda," said Pintacki, his eyes fixed on Hammett, who ignored him and drank his coffee. "First, a permanent, big army in new uniforms, yellow uniforms, symbols of the sun and of the everlasting light and power of the one and indivisible God, visible everywhere, patrolling every few feet of our threatened borders—Canada, Mexico. Second, no taxes. Everybody in the whole damn country gets paid fifteen percent less. The fifteen percent goes straight to the government. The people don't even know it's gone."

"It'll pay for those new yellow uniforms," I said.

"You mock me again, Peters," Pintacki said, pointing at me, "and Wylie will take you outside and turn you into rattlesnake bait. Besides that, you'll miss the show. You wouldn't want that."

"I wouldn't want that," I said.

"We take over every country we beat in the war. Not just occupy it. Take it over. None of this namby-pamby live-and-let-live crapola. Make every country we take over one of the United States. Make them American. Japs, Germans, Eye-talians. Not the A-rabs though. Not the A-rabs. They'd suck us up like the desert and they don't change their clothes. The others . . . give them a vote, representatives, senators, but don't give them too many choices. Most of the whole damned world will be America. And the people in these new states will love it. Love baseball," he said, holding up a finger. "Love hamburgers made with lean, red beef, lots of protein," he went on, holding up a second finger. "Love corn, love Kate Smith, love movies, love everything American."

"Sounds like a great plan," I said.

"Sounds like bullshit," Hammett said, standing up. "I don't listen to bullshit and lunatics, not unless they own movie studios and pay me five hundred dollars a day. Pintacki, you are an extra, unnecessary hole in the rear end of civilization and I just don't have time for you. I should be having my bridgework done and getting a plane east, not sitting in the middle of the desert with an overgrown ten-year-old who wants to play Nero. We've got enough of those in Europe."

Pintacki's face had gone red, then purple and was now white. He stood to face Hammett across the table.

"You are abusing my hospitality," he said evenly. "You are comparing me with Hitler. I hate Hitler. I'd shoot the little paperhanger like a dog if I had him in front of me. I'd tie his dead carcass to a cactus and let his flesh rot and leave his bleached bones to ask God for forgiveness."

"Then I've obviously misjudged you," Hammett said, wiping his mouth with a napkin and putting the napkin neatly next to his plate. "You are a avenging angel, possibly even a saint. Posterity will have to be the judge. Frankly, I've got you fitted for a straitjacket and a red, white and blue padded cell if you live out the season."

Hammett pushed back his chair and went on: "You can shoot me or beat my head in, either of which would allow me the pleasure of knowing that I wouldn't have to listen to any more of your ranting, but I am leaving."

Wylie stepped forward, shotgun now raised and ready.

"It's show time," Pintacki announced. "Sit down."

Conrad, who must have been standing outside the door, came into the room, set up a tripod screen and moved solemnly to the projector.

"Sit down, Mr. Hammett," Pintacki said again. "No more political talk. You've got my word, at least for now. I promised you a show, and by God and the memory of Alexander Hamilton and Saint Sebastian, I'm going to deliver."

"Hammett," I said. "Let's watch a movie."

Hammett looked at me, his face calm but set, his eyes still angry. He sat and so did our host.

"Better," said Pintacki. "People get riled, worked up, without knowing the whole story."

Pintacki pointed to Conrad and sat back. Conrad hurried around closing all the drapes and moved back to his post next to the projector at Pintacki's end of the table.

"It's dark," Pintacki said, "but not too dark for Wylie to see you. You are in for a treat. What do we have this morning, Conrad?"

"*Return of Draw Egan*," Conrad said, hitting the switch. The projector ground into action, a beam of dusty light turned into a rectangle on the wall, and there stood William S. Hart. The cat leaped on the table and went for my plate. I pushed it toward him.

"A favorite of mine," Pintacki said. "One of my bits of immortality. I'm in the gang, get shot in the saloon by Bill. I'll point me out when . . . see that bandana Bill's wearing? I've got it upstairs. Place of honor, framed in my bedroom on the wall where I can see it every morning and remember the values our founding fathers wanted . . ."

"You were an actor?" I interrupted. The cat had finished eating and was looking up at the picture.

"An actor with ears," Pintacki said, tugging at his right earlobe. "I listened, picked up information, figured out what property might be hot, saved my money and bought land. Sold it to the studios for big profits. There, right there, that's Louise Glaum. Went on to be a star on her own. Not my kind, too short, not enough neck, but a decent woman."

The cat prowled along the table toward the image on the screen and when he reached the edge, cocked his head in curiosity and reached a paw toward the nearby screen.

"I respect animals," said Pintacki. "All animals from the smallest flea to the goddam biggest whale, but if that cat touches the screen, Wylie, blow him off hell's hinges."

The cat's paw moved forward and Wylie stepped away from the wall and leveled his shotgun down the table. Hammett reached for the cat and got his hands on him just as Wylie pulled the trigger. Buckshot tore across the top of the table, catching the tip of the cat's tail and tearing into the screen, cutting a character named Arizona Joe into shreds.

"You all right?" I called to Hammett before the echo of the blast and the smell of the shot faded.

"Yes," he said quietly over the voice of Pintacki, who was now bellowing.

"Open the damn drapes . . . hell, I'll do it myself."

Light came back into the room, almost wiping out the picture on the shredded screen. I could see Hammett clearly now. He held the frightened cat to his chest. Blood trickled between his fingers into the cat's orange fur. Hammett spoke softly to the animal.

Wylie stood aiming the shotgun at me and then back to Hammett, ready to fire the second barrel. Conrad stared at Pintacki, waiting for orders, and Pintacki surveryed the damage to the table, screen and wall.

"Should I shoot the cat?" Wylie asked.

"No," said Pintacki. "You had your chance. You missed. Get the Mexican out here this afternoon to work on the wall and table. Hell, let's see the end of the movie."

"I've seen enough movie," Hammett said, standing with the cat in his arms.

"You want a comedy?" Pintacki offered. "I was in *Safety Last*. One of the crowd watching Lloyd. You know, he really did his own stunts. I remember . . ."

"I'm going back to my cell," Hammett said.

"It's your doing," Pintacki said, pointing at Hammett. "We could still have been talking politics. Hell, go to your room. Peters and I will watch the rest."

"I've had enough entertainment for one day," I said, getting up.

"Well," sighed Pintacki, moving around the table and back to his place. "You are less than ideal guests."

"I can't say you're the worst host I've encountered," said Hammett. "You kidnap me, lock me in a room, drag me out to watch an old movie in the middle of the night and shoot me. That's better treatment than I got from the Warner brothers."

"This day is not turning out the way I wanted it," sighed Pintacki.

"I can shoot them, Mr. P.," Wylie offered.

"Can I turn off the projector?" Conrad asked.

"Turn it off," said Pintacki. "Wylie, take them back to their rooms."

We moved toward the door behind the torn screen. I could smell the scorched wood of the table. The pellets in the white wall looked like some constellation of stars, but I didn't know which.

Hammett paused and turned back. "Pintacki," he said, "if you've got a friend, find him and he'll tell you the desert has baked your damn brain."

"How bad is it?" I asked Hammett as we walked into the hallway with Wylie behind us.

Hammett handed me the cat and looked at his hand, turning it around.

"Not bad," he said. "Pellet cut the skin between my fingers. Took the end of the cat's tail. We'll live."

He held out his hand to show me.

"Don't bleed on the floor," said Wylie. "Me and Conrad have to clean it up."

"Sorry," said Hammett, and we walked on.

"Did they bring you straight here yesterday?" I whispered.

Hammett nodded yes.

"And Pintacki was here when you came?"

Another yes.

"Then he lied about not having a phone," I said softly. "He called Spainy just before they grabbed you."

"That's the way I see it," he agreed. "We've got to get to that phone."

"Don't talk and don't bleed," said Wylie behind us as we moved up the stairs.

"He didn't reload," I said, as we neared the first landing and the room I'd spent the night in. "One barrel. Go down low when I move?"

Hammett nodded yes. I stopped suddenly and put the cat down, hoping Wylie would come up at least another step or two before he stopped. He came up two steps. I stretched, turned my head and grinned back at him. He leveled the gun at my chest. I shook my head and gave him a look suggesting he was the nastiest form of life on the underside of a lizard.

"How can you work for a lunatic like Pintacki?" I asked.

"Lot of people are a little nuts," said Wylie. "Doesn't stop them from being presidents or kings."

"I don't know," I said. "I think you have to be more than a little feebleminded to ride along with a peanut-head like Pintacki."

He lifted the shotgun toward my face. That's what I wanted, that and no time to think. I half saw or imagined Hammett going flat on the stairs as I dropped low and threw myself at Wylie's legs. The shot crackled over me as I hit him and we went down the stairs. At first I was on top. After one roll, he was on top. When we hit the bottom of the stairway, we were side by side and dazed. I could see Hammett coming down the stairway toward us, the cat between his legs slowing him down.

Wylie reached for my neck. I tried to scramble backwards, but he grabbed my shirt. There wasn't much time. Conrad and Pintacki had to hear the shotgun blast. They'd be here in a few seconds. I punched at Wylie's face with my left hand and connected with his neck, which was even better. He let go of my throat and gasped for air. I scrambled to my feet as Hammett hit the floor. He picked up the shotgun and kneeled next to the gasping Wylie. Wylie, still choking, tried to stop Hammett from going through his pockets, but Hammett wasn't having any. He pushed Wylie's hands away, reached into Wylie's overalls and came out with two shotgun shells just as Conrad and Pintacki came to the stairs at the carpeted landing farther below us.

"Far as you go," Hammett ordered, aiming the empty gun at the two men, who froze halfway up.

"Bluffing," said Pintacki, "like Mary Pickford in Griffith's *The Londale Operator*. I was in one Pickford film, *Sparrows*."

"I don't think anyone really gives a shit, Pintacki," I said, getting up.

"Not bluffing," Hammett said, holding up one of the shotgun pellet loads he had taken from Wylie.

Wylie tried to catch his breath and actually got something like a word out.

"Don't care," said Pintacki. "Worth a chance to me. Put the gun down or Conrad's going to take out his pistol and shoot you right between the eyes."

"Then I think I'll start by making a lot of holes in Conrad," said Hammett as I moved to his side.

Conrad hesitated, hand on the pistol in his holster. Wylie was on his knees, rubbing his neck.

"Shoot him, Conrad," Pintacki ordered. "Shoot them both. We've got things to do, a world to save and no time for bullshit and bragging."

Still Conrad hesitated. We wanted to get down the stairs and Hammett had put one foot in that direction, the shotgun leveled at Conrad's stomach.

"Shit," muttered Pintacki, reaching over to take the pistol from Conrad's hand.

Hammett and I looked at each other and knew what to do. We turned and jumped for the stairway as Pintacki fired. Wylie made a grab for my leg. I kicked his arms away.

"My hand used to be as steady as a desert rat's dick," wailed Pintacki, clomping up the stairs toward the landing behind us. I led the way, got to the next landing and pushed open the door of my old cell. Hammett, empty shotgun in hand, was right behind me. Pintacki was at the bottom of the flight of narrow stairs. He fired again. This one went between us and tore into the ceiling just over our heads. I slammed the heavy door shut and looked for something to block it with. I went for the nearby dresser while Hammett calmly but quickly broke open the shotgun, dumped the empty shells and inserted the two loaded ones he'd gotten out of Wylie's pocket.

We could hear Pintacki coming up the steps.

"Stop," shouted Hammett. "I've got it loaded now."

"You'll just have to prove that to me," panted Pintacki. "Or we're coming in, and we are damned disgruntled."

Hammett aimed at the door and fired. The pellets thudded into the thick wood.

There was a beat and Pintacki's voice outside came back.

"Wylie tells me you got two loads of shot. That's one. You've only got one left. I'd call this a stalemate."

"We're getting out," I said.

"Don't see how," called Pintacki. "Come out the door and whoever's here will greet you with gunfire. If you're lucky enough to get the draw on him, you'll have to face the rest of us and we'll know for sure that you've got nothing to back yourselves up with. We have both a stalemate and a fiasco, gentlemen. I'm man enough to admit it. This hasn't gone well at all. The man who can admit his mistakes and rise above them is the man who will prevail. But I'll learn from this and go on."

"Pintacki," I said, as Hammett sat on the bed. "You are out of your damn mind."

"Maybe so, maybe no, but I've got the MacArthur papers and you two corked like June bugs in a wine bottle," he said. "We'll just wait it out. I've got till half past forever, if need be. When you get hungry or thirsty, you just call out and we'll make some kind of deal, if I'm in a good mood."

With that he went silent, or seemed to. I went to the door and put my ear against it. I could hear Pintacki's voice whispering but I couldn't make out the words. I pushed the dresser in front of the door and turned to Hammett, who had put down the shotgun and was using his mouth and uninjured hand to fashion a bandage from a piece of bed sheet he had torn from the bed. I gave him a hand.

The cat jumped out from under the bed where he had apparently been hiding and leaped onto the window ledge. His tail wasn't bleeding but it looked just a bit shorter.

"Well," I said, sitting next to Hammett. "What now?"

"You're the boss," he said with a dry smile.

"Okay," I answered. "We get out of this room, find the telephone, call for help, grab the MacArthur papers and get the hell out of here. How do you like it?"

"Fine," said Hammett. "But how?"

"You asked me *what* we're going to do, not *how*. I don't know how."

Outside the door someone padded down the stairs. I wandered over to the window to look out at the desert through the bars. The cat looked up at me and meowed. I didn't feel like playing.

9

About an hour after we pushed the dresser in front of the door, a rifle shot cracked out in the desert, followed by the ping of a bullet against one of the iron bars on the window. A second shot hit the painting of Tom Mix on the far wall, punctuating the portrait right between the eyes. The cat was already gone. He'd rubbed against my leg, looked into my eyes, meowed in anger and, finally, realizing he wasn't getting any water or food out of us, he jumped on the window ledge, squeezed between the bars and leaped into space. Hammett, sitting on the bed, watched while I ran to the window just in time to see the cat roll over in the sand, shake himself off, and head in the general direction of nowhere.

After the cat was gone, Hammett and I had planned our strategy and escape. It took us ten minutes. His plan was to quietly move the dresser, and then to throw open the door and get the first shot off at whoever was waiting. If we got him, we could take his gun. If we missed, we were dead anyway. I didn't like it. There might be two of them on the stairs. They might be hiding or even up the stairs above us. I didn't have a better plan. I was leaning against the wall, trying to figure out a variation on his suicide run, when the rifle shot came.

Hammett went flat and rolled off the bed. I dropped to the floor. We looked at each other. Both of us were in shirt-sleeves and sweating. The desert heat baked the stone walls. There was a big fan in the room but Pintacki had cut off our electricity.

"Well," said Hammett, grinning at me. "We know one of them is out there. Can't be more than two on the stairs."

I didn't answer. I crawled to the window, got up with my back to the wall and peeked out. About forty yards away, well out of shotgun range, Conrad sat in a wooden chair under a bench umbrella. A rifle rested in his lap and what looked like a two-gallon jug rested in the sand next to him, in the shade of the umbrella. I moved over to take a better look. Conrad spotted me and raised the rifle. I was well back against the wall when the second shot came. This one hit the wall outside. A third shot tore into the far wall, splitting a wood panel.

"Pintacki's going to have a hell of a repair bill," said Hammett, getting up.

"Let's do it," I said.

"Let's hold out a few hours," Hammett countered. "They're tense and ready now. They'll ease up, get tired, lazy."

"Maybe," I said, pulling my wet shirt away from my underarms. "And maybe they have a good idea of how long we can hold out without food and water."

"Maybe," he agreed. "Knew a fellow once when I was working for Pinkerton in San Francisco. Name was Dusty Knight. Little guy. Got into the closet of an apartment where the Knock Phillips gang was planning a heist. Dusty got the goods on Phillips but he was trapped in the closet. Couldn't get out till the gang left, and the gang decided to stay right there and keep an eye on each other till they went on a bank job in two days. Closet was hot, dark, not much air. They could have opened it any time, seen him there and dusted Dusty. Dusty just sat there on the floor for three days and nights. Don't ask me what he did about a toilet. Nothing in there but half a pack of Blackjack gum. Dusty finally went a bit nuts on the third day. It wasn't hunger or thirst, mind you. He said that had passed by the second day. It was anger. He sat there blaming everything wrong in his life on Knock Phillips and his gang, even got the idea that they knew he was in the closet and were quietly giggling, pointing at the closet, doing crude imitations of him—Dusty had a slight lisp and a drooping left eyelid. It was too quiet in the room beyond the closet. Dusty got up, quietly moved his legs for about ten minutes to be sure they'd hold him, and went through the door, gun in hand."

Hammett laughed, a dry laugh that turned into a cough.

"What's so funny?"

"Doctors back in the hospital said desert air would be good for my TB."

"What happened to Dusty?"

"Funny thing," said Hammett. "Turns out he was right. Knock did know he was in the closet. Place was empty when Dusty came out. Just a little note telling Dusty to help himself to a beer and a hunk of cheese. Knock and his gang had hit the bank and were on their way to Indiana where they got caught knocking over a five-and-dime."

"There's a point to all this?" I asked.

"At least two," said Hammett. "One, don't be too quick to think you're crazy. Being crazy might be just what you need to save your life. Two, don't wait too long to make your move or there might not be anyone there to move against and you wind up looking like a fool. And right now I'm beginning to feel a little impatient and very crazy."

Hammett got to his knees and checked the shotgun. The morning had already cost him a pound or so he couldn't afford. His sleeves were rolled all the way back, revealing tight, thin arms. I knew he was going for the door.

Before he could move, another shot came from outside, but it sounded different and nothing pinged into the room or hit the outer wall. Someone shouted beyond the door. We could hear feet on the stairs. Hammett got up and angled his way to the window. More shots outside.

I got up and joined him. Conrad had turned and was firing now at a jeep heading toward him from the general direction the cat and I had come from the night before. Someone in the jeep was shooting back at him. Below us, out of our line of vision, a door opened and someone joined Conrad in firing at the advancing jeep.

Hammett and I looked at each other.

"One in the hall," I said.

He nodded and I moved as quickly and quietly as I could to the door and the dresser. Hammett put the shotgun down next to the door and helped me lift and move the dresser. Shots and shouts filled the air outside, covering some of the noise we were making.

"Now," he said, picking up the shotgun.

"Now," I agreed, reaching over to grab the door handle.

I opened it and Hammett stepped out. No one was there. He pointed the gun upward. Nothing.

There was nothing to say. We moved down the stairs slowly, hit the landing. More shots outside. We could hear the jeep's motor grinding as it bounced over the sand. As we went down the second flight of stairs to the front hall we heard a second car start up.

Hammett raised the shotgun when I opened the door. The DeSoto was kicking dust behind it as it rocked down the road. The jeep spun around about twenty yards away. Major Oren Castle was standing in the passenger seat, aiming his rifle at the fleeing DeSoto. He fired. A ping as a bullet hit the fender. Then I recognized the driver. It was J.V., blue-uniformed, her hair falling over her eyes.

"Are you all right?" Castle called, taking a final shot at the distant car.

"Best two days I've had since I tracked down a stolen Ferris wheel," said Hammett, shotgun at his side.

"Toby," J.V. called, turning off the engine and getting out of the jeep. She hurried toward me, stopped, embarrassed. "You're all right?"

"I'm fine," I said, reaching out to touch her cheek. "Desert air agrees with me. Great for the sinuses."

Castle's drawn face was pointed toward the dot of the DeSoto, and I could tell that he was considering a chase. Instead, he put down his rifle and turned to us.

"Orders are to find you, get you back," said Castle, getting out of the jeep.

Hammett was heading toward the house. I put my arm around J.V. and followed him. Castle removed the jeep's key and came after us, alert in case Pintacki and his men returned.

We headed for the kitchen, found food and bottles of cold water in the refrigerator. Castle went in search of the telephone while we ate, drank and got an explanation of the rescue from J.V.

Major Castle had arrived early that morning and had gone directly to police headquarters—where Chief Spainy said he had no idea where Hammett and I were and he wasn't exactly sure of how to get to Pintacki's place. When Castle had left, J.V. had stopped him and volunteered to drive him to Pintacki's on condition that her brother not get in any trouble. Castle wasn't a cop. He had orders and Spainy wasn't part of them. He'd agreed and they had set out on the rescue.

Conrad had started the shooting but he had been no match for Castle. When Pintacki realized that he had been outclassed, in spite of superior firepower, he had piled his bulldog duo into the DeSoto and taken off.

My question was: Had he taken off with the damning MacArthur papers or were they still in the house?

"The papers?" Hammett said, reading my mind.

"The papers," I agreed, and we set out to find them. We went in different directions. In a bedroom I knew was Pintacki's because William S. Hart's bandana was framed on the wall opposite the bed, I found a table filled with framed and autographed photographs of silent movie stars. I stole one of Wallace Beery dressed as a woman. Back in the early twenties, Beery had been a two-reel comic playing an overgrown Swedish maid. I tucked the picture under my arm and went on looking around the room. There was plenty of crackpot literature on the bookshelves along the wall, including piles of thin books written and published by Pintacki. The titles included:

> *American Armageddon: The Quest for a Leader*
>   *after the Apocalypse*
> *Political Sanity and the Inspiration of Hollywood*
> *Yahoo Democracy: It Can't Work*
> *Never Trust an Oriental*
> *One World and All of It America*
> *War and Peace*

Two hours later we met in the dining room, reasonably sure that the papers weren't in the house.

"I should have gone after them," Castle said.

"You had orders," I reminded him.

He nodded.

The generator coughed and went dead and we decided it was time to get out of the castle of Mad King Pintacki. We walked out to the jeep, where we found the cat curled up asleep in the back seat. He looked as if he had found water. J.V. drove, Castle rode shotgun, Hammett and I sat in the back seat. I gave her directions to my car but took her on a slight detour to Andrew Lansing's body.

He was lying on his back looking up at the sun the way I had left him the night before. A small lizard skittered off his leg and burrowed into the ground.

Castle barely glanced at the body. His mind was on other things.

"I'll tell the Chief," J.V. said. "He'll have to put out a bulletin on Pintacki, especially if you sign a kidnapping complaint."

We bounced on, leaving Lansing's body behind us. When we saw the barbed-wire fence and my Crosley right beyond it, J.V. slowed down. Castle got out while the jeep was still moving, pulled a khaki army blanket out from under his seat and ran over to the fence still carrying the rifle. He threw the blanket over the top strand of wire and motioned for J.V. to come ahead. He guided her slowly and expertly over the blanket. The jeep flattened the fence and we jostled over without picking up a flat tire.

I retrieved my jack from under the fence and my keys from where I'd hidden them. Then we had a motorcade back to Angel Springs, J.V. and me in the Crosley right behind Castle driving the jeep with Hammett at his side, rifle in his lap. I could see as they pulled onto the road ahead of us, Hammett was enjoying himself. No doubt about it.

When we got back to Angel Springs and pulled in front of the police station, Spainy and two of his men—including Barry, who had arrested Hammett and me in front of Pudge Stone's house— were waiting for us. Spainy gave J.V. a sour look when she got out of the Crosley with me close behind.

"Find anything, soldier?" he called out with a grin.

"Enough," said Castle. "I'd appreciate your calling in a bulletin on a 1940 DeSoto, blue, California license number 27183. Three occupants. I think you'll want them for questioning in the murder of one Andrew Lansing. You'll find Lansing's body on Pintacki's land, bullet in the back of his head."

"That's right, Chief," J.V. said, stepping forward.

"Pintacki," Spainy said, biting his lower lip and looking at his sister, then at Barry, trying to find a way out of this.

"Pintacki," Castle said again. "And if he and his men are found, I'd appreciate being informed. I'll call to check with you every two hours."

"Every two hours," Spainy repeated. "Couldn't be a mistake here someplace, could there?"

"No," said Castle.

"Didn't suppose," Spainy said, removing his broad-brimmed hat to wipe his brow with a moist handkerchief. "Didn't suppose. Okay, J.V. How's about you get back to work?"

J.V. looked at me and I nodded. She put her hands on both my cheeks and kissed me, mouth open, wet and long. Then she turned to Chief Spainy defiantly and walked past him into the station.

Barry smirked and Spainy turned on him.

"What the hell's so funny, patrolman?" he said.

"Nothing, Chief," Barry said, suddenly sober.

"Unctuous toad," Spainy said. "Look that one up, patrolman."

"I will, Chief," Barry said.

"Like so much mule shit he will," muttered Spainy. And then aloud, "Anything else you folks would like me doing?"

Castle, Hammett and I couldn't think of anything.

"I'll be back sometime," I said, heading for the Crosley.

"Looking forward to your visit," Spainy said. "We'll have a nice chat."

Hammett picked up the cat and got into the Crosley. Hammett and I had left some things at Pudge's house, but neither of us wanted to go back for them. Castle drove the jeep, following us.

Needing shaves and tired, we drove west away from Angel Springs and headed toward the ocean. We stopped once for gas and sandwiches. Hammett didn't say anything, just held the cat in his lap and listened to the radio. Finally, a little before nine-thirty at night—after Ezra Stone went out of his Henry Aldrich character and told us to buy U.S. war bonds and stamps—Hammett reached over and turned off the radio.

"You heard?" he said.

I knew what he was talking about.

"I heard," I said. "Could be some simple explanation."

"Could be," he said. "You think there is?"

"No," I said.

"What are you going to do with it?" he asked, looking ahead toward the blackout-dimmed but still shimmering low outline of Los Angeles.

"Save it till I get dealt a bad hand," I said. "Play it soon if I don't."

Hammett nodded.

I was parked in front of his hotel on Beverly about an hour later. Castle pulled the jeep in behind me. Hammett put the cat down on the seat next to me.

"Can I give you some advice?" I asked, as he started to close the car door.

"Give it," he said.

"Don't go back to Shelly," I said.

"Shelly?"

"The dentist," I said, as Hammett closed the door further to keep the cat from jumping out. "He's a hack, a quack and a butcher."

Hammett smiled, showing ragged teeth that certainly needed a lot of work. "Thanks for the advice. I'll think it over."

"Thanks for the help," I said. "If I don't see you, good luck with the army."

I watched him walk up the hotel steps, turn and wave. The dim light of the hotel's neon sign made him look pale blue. And then he was gone.

"Peters." Castle's voice came from my left through the open window.

He leaned forward and continued. "Follow me."

"Where are we going?" I asked. "I'm tired, hungry and . . ."

"Follow me," he repeated and moved back to the jeep.

I wanted to complain to the cat, but he had curled up and fallen asleep in the front seat still warm from Hammett. Castle pulled in front of me and I followed him, expecting to take the long ride back to Pasadena. I was wrong. He led me up Coldwater Canyon Drive to the top of the hill and made a sharp left into a driveway. About thirty yards down the driveway, we parked in front of a tennis court next to a new two-story house. Behind the tennis court I could see the moon reflected in a swimming pool. Down to the left I could see the lights of the city that never quite went completely off in spite of blackouts and warnings.

"Nice view," I said, following Castle who said nothing.

We were a dozen feet from the door when it opened and two huge, ugly black dogs bounded out barking and showing lots of teeth.

"Stop," Castle commanded and the dogs stopped. One of them skidded about a foot or two but he stopped. Both dogs went silent and I felt my fingernails loosen their hold on my palms.

"Major," came a voice from the dark doorway and a young man in slacks, white shirt and tie stepped out, machine gun in hand.

"At ease, soldier," Castle said.

The young man whistled softly and the dogs turned and ran back into the house. Castle led me through the door. By the time we got in, the young man with the gun and the dogs were gone.

Castle made a right turn through a dimly lit room and moved to a closed door. He knocked and Douglas MacArthur told us to enter.

We entered. Or rather I entered. Castle let me in and remained outside the door.

It was a dining room, but a dining room ready for battle, ancient battle. Eight chairs made of heavy wood with big arms and high backs surrounded a massive table of matching wood. Books and magazines were piled on the table. The walls were covered with banners and mounted weapons: maces, axes, crossbows.

MacArthur stood behind the chair at the head of the table. He was wearing an Oriental kimono with a towel around his neck, smoking a cigarette in a jeweled holder. The General's hair was smoothed back as if he had just stepped from a shower.

I was seeing a different MacArthur.

"Your report, Mr. Peters," he said.

I reported.

"No letters, no money, no papers," he said softly when I had finished.

"Not yet," I said, "but . . ."

"The time for my departure is approaching," he said loud enough to make the dogs howl for an instant before someone quieted them. "If you do not succeed, Roosevelt . . . there are already rumors that I am about to be appointed ambassador to Russia. I must remain in command of the Pacific. The regimented minds of Roosevelt and those who surround him are not flexible enough to handle quickly the changed situation. They want to make war a science when it is actually an art."

"An art," I echoed, when he paused for response.

"An art," he repeated. "Not the mechanistic mania of liberal patronizers of the people. History teaches us that religion and patriotism have always gone hand and hand, while atheism has invariably been accompanied by radicalism, communism, bolshevism, and other enemies of free government."

He looked down at an open book on the table and went on, his voice trembling with rage.

"If we lose this war, and an American boy with a Jap bayonet through his belly and an enemy foot on his dying throat spits out his last curse, I want the name not to be MacArthur, but Roosevelt. I told that to the President and I tell it to you. I can't afford the luxury of rest. I must be driven by outrage and I want that outrage to recharge you with determination. A day, two at the most, is all you have."

There was no handshake this time. MacArthur picked up the open book from the table, walked to the door behind him and left the room.

Back in the hall, Castle was waiting. He asked no questions. I volunteered no information. He walked me to the front door and I went out into the night. I wasn't sure I was recharged by MacArthur's speech but I knew I didn't want another pep talk from the General. That was motivation enough.

The cat opened one eye when I got into the car. Then he went to sleep again. I stopped at a Ralph's Market on the way back home. I picked up some milk, tuna and cold cuts, a new box of Wheaties and a loaf of bread. It was almost eleven when I hit Heliotrope and parked, almost legally, at the corner, half a block away from Mrs. Plaut's boarding house.

There were several ways to handle this. I could hide the cat. I wasn't sure how. He was too big to fit under my Windbreaker and even if he did, I didn't think I could keep him quiet. I could simply carry him in and hope that Mrs. Plaut was asleep or wouldn't hear me. That had worked only once in the time I had lived under her sagging roof. Mrs. Plaut did not sleep.

I picked up the cat, the grocery bag, and the photograph of Wallace Beery, locked the car and walked the half block over and up the stairs. The night was cool and the house dark except for the night light in the hall. Mrs. Plaut's lights were out. I went up the porch stairs as quietly as I could, and the cat cooperated. I made it through the front door and stopped trying to be quiet. Mrs. Plaut was sitting in the straight-backed wooden chair in the hall, wearing a flannel shirt and work pants with a white shawl over her shoulders. Something that may have once been a radio or a secret Japanese radar-beam detector rested in her lap. She was probing it with a screwdriver, her lips tight, her eyes fixed on something inside the box.

I walked toward the stairs, knowing I didn't have a chance but keeping alive the faint spark of hope, a spark that suggested she might be so absorbed in what she was doing that she wouldn't notice me and the cat.

"You have a cat," she said, when my foot hit the first step.

"I do," I admitted, turning to her.

"Is it a he cat or a she cat?" she asked, still probing and lip-pursing.

"A he," I said.

"She cats raise hell and commotion," she said. "Aunt Isabelle had a she cat named Newz, short for New Zealand where Aunt Isabelle claimed her husband had gone, never to return. Aunt Isabelle was fond of sitting on her porch and saying to all and sundry who might question her vigil, 'I am waiting for Newz!' "

"It's a he," I said.

"Prove it," she said.

I put down the grocery bag and the photograph of Wallace Beery and held the cat up under his forepaws, his legs dangling, his maleness demonstrated. The cat looked around and licked his lips.

I was sure he smelled Mrs. Plaut's bird. Mrs. Plaut looked up, craned her neck forward and nodded in acceptance.

"It's a he," she acknowledged. "You can keep him around, providing he stays clean and you feed him."

"I'm not going to keep . . ." I began, but she was back to her screwdriver and had ideas of her own.

"Have you read my M.S.?" she asked.

"Your M.S.?"

"Man-u-scrip," she explained. "Met a woman at the ration board who writes books about pine drops. She said to call it an M.S., man-u-scrip."

"Pine dro . . . I haven't finished your manuscript yet," I said. "Two men have been murdered. I was locked in the tower of a castle in the desert and escaped with the help of an assault by the United States Army."

"Excuses," she said, finally getting some small screw to turn. "Where would my family be if Grandfather Stoltz hadn't joined the wagon train from St. Louis?"

"I don't know." I said.

"Probably Sandusky, Ohio," she supplied pertly.

"I'll have it read by tomorrow," I promised. "I left it in my office before the murders. I've got a new photograph of Marie Dressler."

I retrieved the Beery photo and handed it to her. She let the radio rest in her lap while she examined the photograph.

"You're sure this one is Miss Marie Dressler?" she asked, with suspicion.

"On the set of *Grand Hotel*," I lied.

She frowned at the photograph, seemed ready to ask another question and changed her mind.

"I will place it back on the porch," she said, putting the photograph down next to her chair. "Please do not shoot it again."

"I won't," I promised.

"People have been looking for you," she said, as I tucked the cat under my arm, grabbed the groceries and started up the stairs.

"People?"

"A man with no manners who had a case of the pox when he was a child, and two jesters in overalls who looked like my friend Selma

Rice's dogs," she explained. "I did not like their style. I suggest you seek more amiable friends."

"That is my goal in life, Mrs. Plaut," I said, getting up one more step.

"It will serve you well," she agreed.

"Good night," I said.

"Good night," she said, and moved her nose inside the small black box of screws, tubes and wires.

Since there was no lock on my door, or any of the doors in Mrs. Plaut's boarding house, and since my .38 was probably in the pocket of Conrad or Wylie, I went into Gunther's room next to mine. Gunther was in San Francisco and I was sure he wouldn't mind as long as I kept the place clean. If Pintacki and his men came looking for me, I'd hear them and have time to go out Gunther's window and down the fire ladder against the wall.

I knew Gunther would have some delicacies in his small refrigerator, like gnu liver pâté and pickled quail eggs, but I stuck with what was in the brown bag I placed on a polished table. I vowed to keep away from Gunther's desk and books, and protect whatever I touched. I gave the cat a bowl of milk, which was probably not good for him, and a can of tuna, which looked good to me.

I ate my Wheaties and a Spam sandwich with Miracle Whip, and tried to figure out what my next move might be. It was simple. Pintacki had the MacArthur papers. Pintacki wanted me. I'd make it easy for him to find me and then I'd get him to give me MacArthur's campaign papers. I'd leave the details for later. When I finished dinner, the cat made noises like he wanted to go out. I could have opened the window. I knew he could jump from Mrs. Plaut's second floor, but I didn't know how he could get back in. The hell with it. I opened the window. He went for it, bounded up to the sill, wagged his abbreviated tail, looked out into the night and leaped.

I left the window open, propped one of Gunther's chairs under the doorknob, took off my shoes and lay down on Gunther's sofa—a cousin of the one in my furnished room, except the little doilies on the arms of his were clean and white. I needed a shave, a bath, clean teeth and a new outlook on life. None of them were on the way that night. I closed my eyes and let the automatic part of my brain worry about the return of the cat or Pintacki and his boys.

I slept great. No dreams I can remember, though I had the feeling I had been dreaming when the sound of a door opening woke me. Gunther's chair was firmly in place under the doorknob. The sound was coming from my room. I almost checked my watch but I stopped myself and looked around. Gunther had a desk clock. I rolled off the couch and squinted at it. It was a little after five. Mrs. Plaut wouldn't be in my room for at least another two hours.

I could hear movement in my room, and the sound but not the words of two male voices. I grabbed my shoes and my Windbreaker and went for the open window. As I put one bare foot over the sill and searched for the top rung of the fire ladder, I could hear someone trying Gunther's door. When I'd gone down five or six rungs I could hear someone pushing at the door. When I hit the damp morning ground, I could hear, above me, Gunther's door being forced open and the chair clattering into the room. I ran for the corner of the house and almost made it.

"There he is," I could hear Pintacki say from Gunther's window. This was followed by a bullet cracking through the crisp morning. The bullet hit Mrs. Plaut's cement path behind me.

I got around the corner of the house and heard Pintacki's voice: "Wylie, you have no goddam skill with that weapon whatsoever. Get out in front."

I ran. My back, stiff from sleeping on Gunther's soft sofa, told me to slow down, but my back didn't know what I knew. I kept running, my feet slapping against the asphalt. Birds were chirping and the air felt California moist, green and new. Nothing was on the street but a milk truck that rolled lazily to a stop in front of a house in the middle of the block.

My Crosley was where I'd left it, but the two front tires were flat. Pintacki had covered my retreat. I glanced over at the door of Mrs. Plaut's boarding house in time to see Conrad and Wylie step out on the porch, each of them carrying a pistol.

Pintacki's DeSoto was double-parked in front of Mrs. Plaut's, which gave me an idea. I couldn't outrun them even if my back were perfect. I had no gun. I had no car. I was barefoot. Hiding on Heliotrope wasn't likely. Conrad and Wylie started down the white wooden steps toward me and paused because, instead of running away from them, I was headed down the middle of the street toward Mrs. Plaut's, knowing surprise was my only chance. Once they figured out what I was doing, and I knew from my limited experience with them that it would take some major mental effort on their part, they would cut me off and cut me down before I got the their car.

But before they figured out what was happening, Mrs. Plaut, wearing a blue bathrobe, came running out of the house—clutching over her head in both hands the dying shell of the radio she had been working on the night before.

"Mountebanks," she shouted, bringing the radio down on Conrad's head before he could fully turn and face her. Conrad's knees buckled and he slipped down the steps to the sidewalk. Wylie turned to his partner's aid and aimed his pistol at Mrs. Plaut's head. I was only a few feet from the DeSoto but I stopped, barefoot and panting, wondering if I could get to Mrs. Plaut in time to help her without getting myself killed.

Mrs. Plaut answered my question by bringing her trusty radio shell down on Wylie's arm. A wild shot from Wylie's pistol tore through the screen door into the house. A beat later, Pintacki staggered out, clutching his left shoulder and making a pained face like Our Gang's Alfalfa.

Doors were starting to open up and down Heliotrope. I clutched at the door of the DeSoto. It was open. Not only was it open, they had left the key in the ignition and the motor running for a quick getaway after my murder.

I opened the car door, threw my shoes and Windbreaker onto the front seat, followed them, slammed the door, hit the lock and threw the car into first. The wounded trio headed toward me, Wylie holding his arm, Pintacki holding his shoulder and Conrad staggering in a daze. I gave them a wave and took off down the street. In the side-view mirror I saw Pintacki step into the street. I was hoping he'd be yelling, cursing, raging, but he just stood there bleeding and looking cold and calm as I hit the corner and turned. Mrs. Plaut was on her way down the front steps after the defeated trio.

If there was another battle, I missed it.

10

The DeSoto had a damned good radio. I wondered how much Zanzibar Al would get for it as I turned the corner at Ninth and pulled into the alleyway behind the Farraday. I didn't worry about where I was parking, just pulled over to the side and got out of the car, leaving the door open.

Zanzibar Al emerged from the dark side of nowhere—behind a cardboard box that had once housed a refrigerator—and coughed his way over to me. He had his blue shirt on today and seemed to have found a new rope to hold up his pants.

"Nice vehicle," he said shakily.

"It's yours," I said, throwing him the keys. He put out his bony hands to catch them but they had jangled onto the cracked concrete before he fully grasped that they were coming.

"I'm not a driver," he said, bending down to pick up the keys. "No license of any kind for anything. And nowhere to go."

"Why should you be different?" I said. "It's yours anyway. Push it over in the shade and live in it."

Zanzibar Al looked at the keys, the car, and me. He said softly, "Too much responsibility. I don't want responsibility. I gave it up twenty years back."

"Then sell the tires, the radio, the seats, whatever you find in the trunk," I said, heading for the rear door of the Farraday. I went in without looking back.

Jeremy hadn't turned the night lights off. The place glowed like West Hollywood at night before the war. Since it was a good hour before Jeremy would begin his daily dousing of Lysol, the smell of stale yesterday jittered in the air.

I took the stairs as fast as I could. I hadn't been to the YMCA on High Street for a couple of weeks and it showed. By the time I hit the sixth floor I was winded and looking back over my shoulder. Even someone as dense as Pintacki and the boys would find me before lunchtime. All they would have to do is open the L.A. directory under Investigators, Private, and there I'd be between Parkinson and Pinkerton.

I knew there was someone in the office as soon as I put my key in the outer door; the lock was open. There was no way the Pintacki crew could have gotten here that fast. They had wheels to find and wounds to bind. I should have at least an hour on them, maybe more.

When I opened the inner door past the waiting alcove, I found Shelly stacking his dental magazines in a somewhat neat pile on his instrument case in the corner. He was singing "Sand in My Shoes," and dum-dumming most of the words as he scuttled around, glasses at the tip of his nose, cigar in the corner of his mouth. He heard the door and turned around.

"Good morning, Toby," he said genially. "You look like hell."

"Shelly, it must be seven in the morning," I said.

"More like six-thirty," he said happily. "How you like the clean-up campaign?"

"Long way to go, but impressive. What's going on?"

"Sam, the patient who was in the chair the other day. You remember him?"

"I remember him, Shel," I said, angling toward my office door.

"Listen," Shelly said, taking the cigar out of his mouth and leaning toward me to whisper. "I forgive you for getting him drunk or whatever the hell you did. He'll be back this morning and that's all that really counts."

"Very generous of you, Shel," I said.

"I think he's got money. I quoted him a price to perform magic in his mouth and he didn't flinch," said Shelly, examining a stained bag of cotton swabs and reluctantly dropping them in the garbage. "He's coming back this morning."

"He called?" I asked Shelly, the foe of filth, whose eyes found the sink filled with rusting instruments, sludge-bottomed coffee cups, nightmares of strawberry Danish rolls.

"No, but he has his second appointment this morning," Shelly said. "I got a feeling things are going my way. And, you know what?"

"No," I said.

"Mildred called," he said with a grin, returning the cigar to his mouth and reaching for the back of his dental chair, where his stained, once-white smock lay. "I'll call her back later. Give her time to think."

"Good strategy," I said.

"Probably wants me back," he said, putting his head and pudgy arms through the smock. "I plan to think about it. Make her sweat in her own juice. Did I tell you about Louise-Marie?"

"You mentioned something about hiring a dental assistant," I said.

"Louise-Marie Fursthomer," he said, pausing to tap a drill bit against his palm and imagine Louise-Marie. "A very professional woman. She'll be coming in later today for an interview. That ought to get Mildred thinking."

"Good plan, Shel. So you're cleaning up for your new patient and a dental assistant. You have my blessing. Now, I've got work to do," I said. "Three guys are looking for me, want to kill me. I stole their car and got one of them shot."

"That can wait," Shelly said, his head popping out of the smock he was putting on. "I'm talking about something important here, Toby. I'm talking about saving a marriage, Mildred's and mine. The world is in a terrible state of chaos. Here, look."

He grabbed a crumpled morning *Los Angeles Times* from his dental chair and held it up.

"There's going to be a national thirty-five-mile speed limit," he said. "The Nazis look like they're going to take Stalingrad. But am I crying? Am I down?"

"Not yet," I said, reaching over to take the newspaper. There was an article on the front page with a bulletin from General Mac-Arthur's headquarters in Australia, saying that the Japanese drive in

New Guinea had been halted, but the General himself had been too busy to make himself available for comment.

"Are you crying?" Shelly asked brightly. "Crying from the pathos of the world?"

"Not yet," I said, hanging the paper back to him.

"Then what the hell," he said, with a yellow-toothed grin ill-becoming a doctor of dental surgery. "I read the chapter you gave me, Mrs. Plaut's book." He hurried over to the file cabinet, fished around and came back with a thick envelope. "That woman can write. Got to give her credit. I always thought she was just a batty old fart."

"I'm sure she'll be happy to hear that," I said, taking the envelope.

"I've made some comments, suggestions," he said. "The business about her great-aunt's marrying three Indians from different Sioux tribes is hot stuff."

I tucked the envelope under my arm.

"Shel, those guys I told you about might be here any minute to kill me. I've got to get going."

"Okay, okay," he said, throwing up his hands. "I try to cheer you up, share a little good news and hope, and all you can think about is your problems. I've got work to do here anyway."

I hurried into my office, closed the door. I didn't have to turn on the light. The morning sun was bright and dancing off the building next door. I opened the envelope and placed Mrs. Plaut's pages on the desk, threw open the window and heard the echoing voice of Zanzibar Al arguing with someone out of sight below me. I made a few phone calls and decided to pull out twenty bucks of Mac-Arthur's money I had hidden in a copy of *The Collected Tales of Ambrose Bierce* in my bottom drawer.

The twenty was there, but Major Oren Castle wasn't at the number he had given me. Someone answered and said they'd give him the message as soon as they could find him. The message was simple—*help*. I was willing to sit in my office and draw the bears but I needed someone standing behind them when they stepped into it. Castle, I knew from firsthand experience, was handy with a gun.

In the other room, Shelly turned on the radio and listened to "The

Romance of Helen Trent." Helen was leaving desperate phone messages for someone named Hanson. I had my own problems. I made another call, a just-in-case call, to a twenty-four-hour-a-day number I had written along with half a dozen others on the center drawer of my desk—just under my inadvertent collection of lint, paper clips and shoelaces.

"Is Wolfy there?" I asked.

"Talk," barked Wolfy.

"It's Toby Peters. I need a weapon."

"Handgun?"

"Right."

"Legal?"

"Right."

"When?"

"Now."

"Twenty-five for a nice little Luger, very German," said Wolfy.

"Twenty," I countered.

"Join the German army. They'll give you one free and lots of live targets."

"Twenty is all I've got with me," I said.

"People think I'm Santy Claus."

"You're a saint. Saint Wolfy the first," I said.

"I got no religion, Peters. Where are you?"

"My office in the Farraday."

"My man will have it there, loaded, in ten minutes. You give him the twenty and he hands it to you."

"Thanks," I said.

"Hey, it's business," replied Wolfy and hung up.

I could have used a bowl of Wheaties or a Danish and coffee. I couldn't go for them so I settled on a shave. I kept an extra Gillette razor in the drawer, along with a packet of Blue Blades. I fished it out, had a fleeting thought of the cat, and went back into Shelly's office. He was plugging away at the sink, filling the garbage can rather than cleaning the cups and instruments. The garbage can was overflowing on the floor—bloody cotton, coffee grounds, a broken rusty probe.

"I'll get new stuff," he said, holding up a white bowl which neither of us recognized despite its flower pattern and the residue of brown something at the bottom. Shelly tossed it on top of the garbage pile, where it teetered and then came to rest.

I grunted and reached over his shoulder for our bar of soap, which was down to a nub the size of my thumb.

Behind us Helen Trent reached Hanson and gushed that she was so relieved to find him. I turned on the hot water and shaved without a mirror, marveling at the unfamiliar sight of the bottom of the sink which winked at me from between the last dozen or so items congealed there.

"He's late," Shelly said, looking at his watch as he picked up the paper and sat in the dental chair, keeping an eye on the door. "Hell, so he's late. He'll be here, right?"

"Any good news in the paper?" I asked, continuing to shave, nicking my cheek on a rough patch where the cat had scratched me on our first meeting.

"British have a new drive on Madagascar," he muttered. "I don't even know what Madagascar is."

I left Shelly to his radio soaps and went back into my office, figuring about five minutes had passed. Should be plenty of time, I thought. I thought it, but I was wrong for the first time in my life. Well, maybe not the first time.

My first thought when I heard Shelly's outer door open was that Hammett had ignored my advice and prepared to lay himself once again on the altar of the Hatchet Man of Hoover Street, but it wasn't Hammett. I heard a familiar man's voice through the door. I sat back in my chair, put my feet up on the desk and my hands behind my head, and put on a smile that claimed to know something very special and secret. And then the door flew open.

Conrad and Wylie stepped into the already crowded office. Now that I was close to it, I could see that the gun in Wylie's left hand was my .38. I didn't know who owned the gun in Conrad's hand. Wylie's right arm was in a sling. Conrad's head bore a bandage, a neat cross of a bandage that appeared to be covering a wound in his head. Mrs. Plaut had done her duty but it hadn't slowed down these troops. Between Conrad and Wylie stood Shelly, Conrad's thick fingers around his neck holding him out like a ventriloquist's dummy; only this dummy was turning red in the face and about to lose his glasses.

"Cops are outside," I said.

"Like so much shit," spat Wylie.

"Shit," echoed Conrad.

"How about an old lady with a radio," I tried. "She's on the way up."

"You think you're funny? We'll show you funny. Mr. Pintacki said do what we have to do, and then we can do what we want to do. You know what I want to do?" Conrad asked.

"Become a hairdresser," I guessed.

Shelly gasped.

"I want to throw you out that window, shoot your face, kick your stomach in, tear out your heart," he hissed through clenched teeth.

"I think you should rearrange the order or you'll miss out on some of the fun," I said, stalling.

"Give it over, now," said Wylie.

Some of the desperation left me. Shelly was sputtering but we had some hope. They hadn't just come to get rid of me. They wanted something they thought I had, and I was pretty sure of what it was. It changed things around, but I could deal with it.

"I give it to you and you throw us out the window," I said. "Not much in it for us."

Shelly struggled to get free but Conrad pinched the dentist's cheek.

"We'll throw you out second," Wylie offered. "Mr. Pintacki wants the papers."

"I'll bring them to him," I said, starting to get up. "Where is he?"

Wylie poked the gun at my chest in warning.

"No," said Wylie. "He said for us to bring it, not you. He's not happy with you."

"Sorry to hear that," I said, "but . . ."

"No buts," shouted Wylie, leaning over the desk and putting the barrel of my pistol against my forehead. Even he wouldn't miss at that distance.

It was at that moment the door to Shelly's office opened again. There was a pause, some footsteps, and the door to my office swung slowly inward. Wylie put his gun into the sling on his right arm and Conrad let go of Shelly's neck. Shelly collapsed into my guest chair, his face looking like a cinnamon heart.

A Negro man about my age, with a paunch and wearing a green sports jacket that didn't come near matching his blue slacks, stepped in carrying a small package under his arm. He was a pro. He didn't look left or right at Conrad or Wylie, who watched in confusion. The man simply ignored the panting Shelly.

"Cash," he said, looking across the desk at me with determined dark eyes.

I handed him the twenty. He passed over the package and left, closing the door quietly behind him.

"Book of the month," I said. "Office delivery."

"The MacArthur papers," said Wylie, retrieving his gun from the sling. "Hell with books."

I tore open the package carefully and pushed my right hand into it, looking over at the frightened, panting Sheldon Minck. I found the barrel of the Luger and decided to take the risk. I lifted the package in my left hand and let the pistol drop out into my right. I aimed it directly at Wylie's left eye.

Shelly finally found his voice and groaned, "I'm too old for this."

Wylie, however, didn't waver. "I'm not scared," he said. "Conrad's not scared."

I wasn't sure about Conrad. I couldn't turn to see him but hysteria was the closest I could come to describing what I saw on Wylie's face.

"So what do we do?" I asked. "Shoot each other?"

"I guess," said Wylie, resigned.

"I thought Pintacki wanted the MacArthur papers," I said.

"That's right, Wylie," Conrad agreed.

"That's right," croaked Shelly, without knowing what we were talking about.

The Luger in my right hand was aimed directly at Wylie. I grasped Mrs. Plaut's chapters, and held them up.

"Let's deal," I said.

Wylie's eyes were not in a dealing mood but he wasn't too far gone yet to forget what he had come for.

"Deal, Wylie," Conrad urged.

"My arm is busted 'cause of him," whined Wylie. "Conrad, don't you know we have been humiliated? You got no pride or something?"

I reached back to the open window with the envelope and dangled it outside.

"What are you up to?" Wylie asked.

"Here's the deal," I said. "I'm dropping the MacArthur papers out the window. They'll go flying all over the place, but you might be able to get it all together if you hurry. I'm counting to three and and then I'm dropping the envelope. You can start shooting or go out the door and down the stairs and see if you can put it all together."

"Hold it," hissed Wylie.

Shelly groaned.

"One," I said with a grin.

"I want to shoot him," Wylie said, fluttering his slung arm like a broken wing.

"We can do that later," Conrad said.

"Two," I went on, my Luger aimed just above my .38 in Wylie's hand.

"It started like . . . I don't know, such a good morning," Shelly said to Conrad.

"Three," I said and I dropped the pages.

"Shit," cried Wylie. He backed toward the door, unable to grab for the knob with one hand in a sling and the other holding my gun. Conrad reached back and threw the door open. I kept my pistol leveled at Wylie's chest. I could see him considering a shot and then giving in. "Not over," he said and following Conrad out, running.

When we heard the outer door bang open, Shelly said, "That was Mrs. Plaut's book. Why the hell do they want to kill you to get Mrs. Plaut's book? It's good but it's not that good."

I reached for the phone and dialed the police. I told them two guys in overalls and carrying heat were in the alleyway behind the Farraday, throwing Nazi propaganda leaflets and shouting "Heil Hitler." I told him the two were shooting at the peace-loving tenants of the building, and to prove it I fired a shot through the window. I screamed once in mock agony for good luck and hung up.

"Toby, what the hell is going on?"

"Secret stuff, Shel," I said, looking out the window. The last sheets of Mrs. Plaut's chapter were coming to rest on the grease and grime of the alleyway. Zanzibar and a few of his pals, who were busily pulling the seats out of the DeSoto, paused to gather in stray pages.

"I'm a dentist," groaned Sheldon Minck. "How does this kind of thing look to my patients? If Sam comes in and . . ."

"I don't think Sam's coming," I said, as Conrad and Wylie dashed through the Farraday's back door and surveyed the mess of manuscript pages. Wylie started by ripping sheets out of the hands of Zanzibar Al and his boys. Conrad kneeled and gathered them in. He looked a little dizzy, probably delayed reaction from the bashing in by Mrs. Plaut, as formidable a toyweight as any who ever trod the canvas.

"Not coming . . ." Shelly sputtered.

"They're not reading it," I said, pleased. Conrad and Wylie didn't even glance at the sheets. They had too much to do and didn't know how much time they had to do it. Also, they may not have been able to read.

"They're saving it for a cocktail and a warm bath," sighed Shelly.

Shelly joined me at the window to watch Wylie and Conrad, with some unrequested assistance from one of Zanzibar Al's boys, who seemed confused about whose side he was on. They had gathered the final sheets when the siren squealed somewhere in the direction of Alvarado.

The keys to the DeSoto were in the car door. Wylie got in the passenger side. Conrad grabbed the keys and got in the driver's side.

The engine turned over, the DeSoto backed into a brick wall, then shot down the alley, narrowly missing Zanzibar Al himself, who danced out of the way. The police car caromed down from the other end of the alleyway and Zanzibar's crew pointed in unison at the retreating DeSoto. The cops paused, saw them and shot out after the fleeing pair.

The alley went quiet and Al looked up at me.

"I'm sorry," I shouted. "About the car."

"I am not," he gargled back. "Material goods. You become attached to them. They've relieved me and we have relieved them."

Zanzibar Al pulled the DeSoto radio from behind his back.

I put in a call to No-Neck Arnie the mechanic, who tried to convince me to apply for a C gas-ration book so he could make a deal with me for the coupons I didn't use.

"Here's how it's going to work," Arnie said, while I listened to the siren pull farther and farther away. "An A book will have a year's supply of coupons, giving 2,880 miles of driving on the basis of four gallons of gas to a coupon. You follow?"

"No."

"Try," he said. "That's based on the government's official estimate of 15 miles to the gallon. Of the total, 1,080 are supposed to be for family driving and 1,800 for the job."

"Fascinating, Arnie," I said.

"A B book," he went on, "will be for drivers whose job requires more than 1,080 miles per year. Trouble is you gotta agree to share the car, but how's the government to know?"

"They won't," I said.

"Right. Now, the C book," he said, getting into it. "That's for drivers who fall into fourteen classifications of essential occupations involving driving more than 470 miles a month. You get ninety-six coupons every three months, good for four gallons a coupon."

"But you have to pay for the gas," I said, trying to get into this because with a war on it paid to be nice to your mechanic.

"Sure, but what I'm talking here is you applying for an occupational allowance. You and Minck both. I'll take the extra coupons off your hands for a fair price."

"I'll think about it," I said, but I knew I wouldn't think about it. I knew if I did it I'd have dreams of jeeps full of soldiers in some jungle running out of gas because I picked up a few bucks from No-Neck Arnie. "Arnie, my car's a half block down from my house, front tires flat. Can you pick it up, fix it, and bring it to your place?"

"Sure," he said. "Twenty bucks. Ten if you think seriously about applying for a C coupon."

"I'll pay the twenty," I said.

"Suit yourself," he said with a deep sigh to let me know what I'd be missing. "You can pick it up here after four."

I hung up, gave a sigh of my own, and tried to figure out the least awkward way to walk down the street and hail a cab with a loaded oversized Luger in my pocket.

11

Shelly wouldn't talk to me. He sat in his dental chair sulking behind the morning paper.

He had been choked, humiliated and kept in the dark. The patient he had started to clean up for, Dashiell Hammett, probably wasn't coming. With good reason, Sheldon Minck assumed it was all my fault.

"They won't come back, Shel," I said. "They know I'll get out of here. Besides, I'll have them nailed by the end of the day if the cops don't catch them now."

A distant siren suggested that the cops hadn't caught up with Wylie and Conrad, which didn't say much for the Los Angeles Police Department since Conrad was driving with a concussion. But, then again, the police had lost most of their youngest and sharpest to the armed forces.

Shelly grunted and rustled his paper. A puff of angry cigar smoke curled over the top of the pages.

"I'll check in later," I said. "You'll have to interview Louise-Mary without me."

"Louise-Marie," he corrected.

"Louise-Marie," I amended. "Mildred will hate her."

To this he did not even grunt. I went down to the sixth-floor landing of the Farraday. It was still early. Most of the tenants—baby photographers, pornographers, fortune tellers, correspondence-school operators, assorted quacks, hacks and shysters—wouldn't be arriving for a while, but I could tell from the aroma of fresh Lysol that Jeremy or Alice or both were on the job. I followed the scent and found Jeremy on the fourth floor just outside the door of a small-time bookie named Desnos Lyme. The sign on the door read: LYME AND ASSOCIATE, INVESTMENTS.

Jeremy kneeled next to the door, bucket on one side of him, Lysol bottle on the other, chamois in hand. He wore a clean red-flannel shirt and dark slacks and, in the demi-darkness of the early-morning windowless interior of the Farraday core, enough light came from the bulbs to shine off Jeremy's shaved head. He had worked his weight down to about 250 pounds, but he still looked like an intelligent mountain.

"Jeremy," I said. "I need a favor."

Jeremy paused. He took a beat to change roles from landlord to friend, but just a beat.

"Yes," said Jeremy, eager to get back to his battle with the inevitable grime of the Farraday.

"A pair of minor-league menaces named Conrad and Wylie just broke into my office, pushed Shelly around a little and waved a gun. It's part of a case I'm on. I don't think they'll come back but I'd like you to keep an eye on Shelly for the rest of the day just in case. You can't miss these two; one has his arm in a sling, the other has a patched head. They always wear overalls. And they're both big, not as big as you, but big."

Jeremy didn't answer. He simply nodded.

"Thanks," I said.

"Toby," he said, as I turned to leave. "The hourglass of life is dropping its silent sand. We must savor each grain and be careful not to crack the glass."

"Comforting thought, Jeremy," I said, taking a step toward the stairs. My footsteps echoed below.

"You miss my point," said Jeremy. "I was not making an existential observation."

"Sorry," I said, not even worrying about what he meant.

"Whatever life is, and I am inclined at least poetically to consider it a continuum, a river of being in which the essence of energy—energy which includes you and me—must flow, will flow and has flown since the beginning of time."

"Gotcha," I said, taking another step.

"No," he went on, "my point is that in this present existence in present time we should honor life and not insult it. Too often you insult it. It is time to consider reflection and contemplation, Toby. You are of an age."

"I'll think about it, Jeremy," I said, finally getting to the stairs. "Meanwhile . . ."

"If those two show up and cause trouble," Jeremy said, reaching down for his Lysol, "I'll crush their heads like ripe pomegranates."

"I'd appreciate that. How's Alice?"

"Pregnant," he said.

I stopped and turned around to face him. I'd never thought of the enormous Alice as a mother. In fact, I'd never thought about how old Alice Pallice Butler might be. I knew Jeremy had to be at least sixty.

"Congratulations," I said.

"A new hourglass to be shined, protected and savored," he said. His face was shadowed but I could see the small hint of what might have been a smile on his usually expressionless face. "To create a new life is poetry but too few of the poets recognize their aesthetic powers."

"When's the baby due?" I asked.

"May," he said.

"These are hard times for having a baby," I said.

"When were the easy times? When were the right times? When were the best times?" He was back to cleaning the walls, and a new wave of Lysol aroma wafted toward me from the open bottle. "You too are capable of poetry, Toby."

"Not so's you'd notice," I said. "I'll leave it to you and Alice. I really am happy for you, Jeremy."

"I believe you are. Now if you and the world will survive long enough to meet my child, I will be very pleased."

I left Jeremy to his endless chore and hurried down the polished stone steps and along the ornate black-painted metal railing, remembering the time I had seen Jeremy calmly throw a crazed giant thirty years younger and thirty pounds heavier across the waiting room of a veterinarian's office. There had been no joy in it for Jeremy, just something he could do and had to do to save my life. He had read me his poetry for years and never shown the slightest emotion other than a resigned melancholy. Even his marriage to Alice had been sober, but I had just seen the touch of a smile on that corded face and it made me feel vulnerable and just a little scared.

My plan was simple. Pintacki didn't have the MacArthur papers. I had some idea of who might have them, but no idea of why. I needed a car.

There were probably ways to borrow a car and better places, but I caught a cab on Hoover and told him to drive me to Culver City. I watched the city wake up as we went west on Pico, cut down Hill and turned a few blocks short of the M.G.M. Studios to the street where Ann lived. I looked around for Ann's car before paying the cabbie, got a receipt and let the cab go. Her shining little black Ford was parked on the street behind a not-so-bright Chrysler.

I didn't bother to check my watch as I walked across the courtyard and past the pond. I figured it was still early. I knocked and waited. I knocked again and finally heard soft footsteps padding and a voice answer dreamily, "Who is it?"

"Toby," I said.

The pause was half of forever, the time it would take for a butterfly's wings to wear down a bowling ball. Then the chain inside clanked, the handle turned and the door opened a crack. Her thick hair was falling over her eyes and she was wearing a blue and white silk robe she had bought when we were still married. Her eyes were a bit puffy but she looked soft and warm.

"How did the interview go?" I asked.

The crack didn't widen.

"Fine," she said. "I got the job."

"Great. Can I come in?"

"I . . . I'm sorry. I've got to get up and get to work."

"Well, you can tell me about the job while you get dressed," I said amiably.

"I'm sorry," she said. "You should have called."

"Too early in the morning. I didn't want to wake you."

"Toby, please . . ."

"Can I borrow your car for a few hours?" I asked.

"My . . . no . . . I need it to . . ." she stammered.

"I'm on this case," I started to explain. "Vital to the war effort. Two guys . . ."

"I don't want to hear, Toby," she whispered. "I don't want to know about your cases. We're not married, remember? I don't have to know. I don't have to wonder. I don't have to worry. I don't have to be responsible for you. You are two husbands ago, Toby. I appreciate what you've done for me but let's just stop it here."

"Yesterday . . ." I began.

". . . was yesterday," she concluded. "Toby, I've got to get ready for work and you can't come in."

"Annie," I said. "Just give me . . ."

And then I heard the cough inside her apartment, over her shoulder, back toward where I remembered the bedroom was. The cough was deep, confident, masculine. Ann heard it too. She chewed on her lower lip, brushed her hair back and looked in my eyes, without apology but with some embarrassment.

"Annie, Annie was the miller's daughter," I said, the song I used to sing to her in my comic voice when we were first married. "Far she wandered from the singing water. Idle, idle Annie went a-maying, uphill, downhill with her flock astraying."

She closed the door quickly and I turned to leave. I didn't really feel like finding murderers and MacArthur's papers. I didn't feel like saving the Western world from the postwar threat of communism. I felt like going to a hotel, getting in bed, pulling the covers over my head and sleeping for a month.

I told myself I didn't care, shouldn't care. After all, I'd spent some time in bed with J.V. in Angel Springs. I'd done it partly because she reminded me of Ann, but I'd also done it out of need, hers and mine. I shouldn't judge Ann. I shouldn't, but I knew I would. I gave up the idea of going for the hotel and decided instead to wait outside of Ann's apartment to get a look at whoever it was in the bedroom. I wasn't sure it would make things better but it would get rid of some of what I would soon start imagining. Before I could turn away, Ann's door opened again, just a crack, and again slammed shut.

"Ann," I called.

There was no answer this time.

"Phil was right again." Seidman's voice came from over my shoulder.

I turned around and found myself facing the pale and placid Lieutenant Steve Seidman.

"About what?" I asked, following him out from behind the palms and cactus.

"About where to find you," he said. "When in doubt, go to your ex-wife's. Let's go."

And we went. Seidman said nothing on the trip to the Wilshire Station. He drove and I looked out the window feeling sorry for myself and wondering if it was going to rain. He parked his unmarked Ford in the small lot and walked with me around the stone building to the front, up the steps and into the lobby.

"What kind of a morning is it?" I asked Seidman.

"Don't know," he said as we walked past the ancient sergeant on duty at the desk, whose face turned sour in greeting. "He called me at home and told me to have you here when he got in."

"You were lucky to find me," I said as we went up the dark, wooden steps toward the squad room.

"You left an easy trail," he said. "Give me a minute with him."

"Take your time," I said, following Seidman through the squad room door. The grimy clock on the wall read almost nine, which meant a shift had changed within the hour. A pair of handcuffed Oriental boys sat on chairs in front of the desk of John Cawelti, a sergeant who didn't love me. John wasn't there. The Oriental boys were leaning against each other. One of them was sleeping. As we passed I could see that the wide awake and frightened boy was really a girl who looked at me as if I might have a reprieve for her, or at least some hope. I had neither.

Another cop, a horsey guy whose name I couldn't remember, sat at his desk in the corner near the dirty window smoking a cigarette and staring at a sheet of paper in front of him. The rest of the squad room was empty, at least empty of humans. The trash cans were overflowing with last night's reports and ordered-out sandwiches and the place smelled like the Griffith Park lion house.

We maneuvered around the desks to Phil's old office in the corner, the rat hole he had crouched in for a dozen years before his promotion and to which he had now been sent back. Seidman pointed to the scratched wooden chair outside the door. I sat. He knocked and went in. I tried to avoid the eyes of the Oriental girl, who looked at me across the squad room over the head of the young man dozing on her shoulder. I tried to avoid her eyes but I couldn't. I shrugged, held my hands up as if they were handcuffed and pointed to myself in an attempt to let her know that she and I were in the same boat. She nodded sadly as if she understood and turned her head away, letting her cheek touch the hair of the sleeping young man.

Phil's door opened and Seidman stepped out. He looked at me but his pale, emotionless face told me nothing. I got up and went in. Seidman stayed outside and closed the door.

Phil was standing at the barred, narrow window behind his desk. The office was only a little bigger than my own in the Farraday, but Phil's presence took and needed more space. His shirt was starched fresh and white, his tie dark and unwrinkled, his face neatly shaved, his short steel-gray hair brushed back. In his right hand was a steaming cup, in his left the remains of a sandwich on white bread.

"Hungry?" he asked.

"Yeah," I said warily.

"Have a seat and a sandwich," Phil said, looking over his shoulder at me and nodding at the paper bag on his desk. "Ruth made three of them for my lunch but I missed breakfast. I'll pick up something at the Greek's later."

I moved around the two chairs in front of the desk and reached into the paper bag for a sandwich. It was wrapped in crinkly brown paper and smelled good. Ruth was good with food and kids.

"Spam," Phil said, going back to the fascinating view of the wall across from his window.

I sat down and opened the sandwich.

"You want a coffee?" he asked, still not looking at me. "I can have Steve get one for you."

"No thanks," I said, starting on the sandwich but eating it like a wary chimp who expects someone or something to try to snatch it from him. Phil was being too calm. "How's it feel to be back in here?"

"Comfortable," he said. "Like home."

"Ruth and the kids okay?" I asked, not sure whether I was trying to provoke him and whether I was really interested.

"Fine," he said. "Told her I'd be seeing you. She wants you to come for dinner Sunday. Three o'clock."

"I . . . I'll be there," I said. "Good sandwich."

"Dave and Nate asked about you, and Lucy's talking a lot," Phil said.

He finished his sandwich and let me finish mine before he turned, clenched his teeth and began.

"Two days," he said. "What have you got on the Hower murder?"

"Another murder," I said. "Andrew Lansing."

"Hower's roommate," said Phil, sitting at his desk and placing his cup in front of him.

"Right," I said. "Police found him on the estate of a guy named Pintacki in Angel Springs. My guess is Pintacki killed Hower and Lansing."

"Why?" he asked, reasonably.

I shrugged. Keeping MacArthur out of this was part of the job.

"Money, I suppose," I said. "I have information that Lansing had a pile of cash."

"Where'd he get it?" Phil asked.

"Client of mine," I said.

"And you want the money back, for your client?" he said calmly.

"Right," I said.

"You don't suppose your client might shoot Hower and Lansing to get his or her money back and not tell you?" he asked.

"No," I said.

"Think you might like to tell me now who this client is so I can talk to him?" he asked, reaching for his cup.

"Phil, you want Pintacki and his two boys. Their names are Conrad and Wylie, and . . ."

". . . they were found dead, shot on a little street off Coldwater Canyon about twenty minutes ago," he finished.

"Pintacki," I said.

Phil didn't look convinced.

"Call Chief Spainy in Angel Springs," I said. "He knows."

Phil reached for the phone and told someone to get Chief Spainy in Angel Springs on the phone. He held the receiver to his ear and we said nothing while we waited. I wanted the third sandwich but I didn't ask for it or suggest that we split it. I have some sense of timing.

"Spainy? This is Captain Phil Pevsner, L.A.P.D. I'm calling about a murder in Angel Springs, a man named Lansing found on the property of someone called Pintacki . . . right . . . okay . . . spell that, please . . . right. I've got two more bodies here, tentatively identified as Wylie Simms and Conrad Stock. Source here says they work for Pintacki . . . I see . . . right . . . thanks."

He hung up and looked at me.

"Spainy has quite a vocabulary," he said.

"He works at it a lot harder than he does at being a cop," I said. "And he's got a thing about rabbits."

"Spainy didn't say anything about rabbits, but he did say Lansing's body was found on the road south of Angel Springs, nowhere near Pintacki's place. He says Pintacki's a law-abiding citizen. The Chief says that he knows nothing about two men named Wylie and Conrad who work for Pintacki."

"He's lying," I said.

"You've got some evidence, someone who can back you up?" asked Phil.

All I had was Hammett, Castle, J.V. and Spainy's man Barry. I'd caused J.V. enough trouble and I owed Hammett a head start to the East Coast. Major Oren Castle was, in a sense, my client. To name him would lead to a clear line to MacArthur.

"No," I said.

"You didn't happen to shoot this Wylie and Conrad, did you?" Phil asked.

"No," I said.

"Steve says you've had a busy morning," Phil went on, pausing to sip from his cup. "Two men showed up at your boarding house shooting and being less than pleasant. Your landlady thinks they're Nazis. From the description, I'd say they're our boys in Coldwater, Wylie and Conrad."

"I wasn't there," I said.

"You weren't there," said Phil pleasantly. "How about an hour later at your office? You drove into the alley in the DeSoto they were found dead in. Minck says the two now deceased came to your office, waved their guns and threatened to kill you. He thinks they were bill collectors."

"Maybe I need a lawyer," I said.

"Maybe you need a new goddam brain," Phil went on, his voice still even but showing a slight quiver that only a brother would recognize. "I've got four connected murders and you know what connects them? You. You connect them, Toby. You are—and not for the first time, as any assistant district attorney will see when he looks into your hippo-choking file—a murder suspect. We're talking possible indictment. We're talking loss of license."

"I didn't kill anyone, Phil. This is all circumstantial."

"Circumstantial is what gets most murderers the death penalty," Phil explained. "I'm trying to keep even here, Toby. The day's just starting. My stomach is full and I'm back in investigations where I want to be, but you are not going to make my first day a disaster."

He stood up and heaved the almost-empty coffee cup past me into the corner, where it shattered. It was a good sign. He hadn't thrown the cup directly at me and he had finished most of the coffee.

"What's going on, Toby? Now, and straight."

He ran his left hand over the top of his bristly hair, which was not a good sign. I had a client to protect. I also had my body to protect and I had the sudden flash of an hourglass, Jeremy's hourglass, with not all that much damn sand left in the top.

"Off the record, Phil," I said. "It has to be off the record."

"No," he said.

"Then I can't tell you." I said, hands at my side ready to protect myself from what would probably be my brother's next move.

"Son of a bitch," he hissed, fists clenched.

"I can't, Phil," I said. "I've got an office smaller than a broom closet, a furnished room in a seedy boarding house, no wife, no family, no money, no property. All I've got is my word. If I give that up, I've got nothing left. I can't tell you, Phil."

Phil's face went red and the first drops of perspiration began to dot his rapidly wilting shirt. He pounded once on the desk with his right hand and sat down.

"Off the record," he agreed. "But you'd better give me all of it."

I gave him all of it including MacArthur, Castle, the missing papers and the money. I didn't give him Hammett's name and I didn't tell him about J.V.

Phil listened quietly, his face growing serious and calm as I went through the tale right up to the moment Seidman's hand touched my shoulder in front of Ann's apartment.

"I was in the Rainbow Division in the war," Phil said quietly when I had finished.

"I know, Phil," I said.

"MacArthur was the C.O. He turned a collection of random militias from all over the country into a proud unit," Phil said softly. "I would have died for that man. I almost did."

Phil had been wounded during the war and had almost died. He'd never talked about what had happened and I could see that he was having trouble with it now.

Phil stopped talking, looked at me and made a decision.

"America needs MacArthur," he said. "Not just for the war but after, when my kids are growing up, when everyone starts getting soft again and someone else decides to stick a knife in our back so that Nate and Dave have to go out and fight and maybe get killed. America needs Douglas MacArthur."

I wasn't as sure about that as my brother was, but this wasn't the time to debate it.

"So," I said. "What do we do?"

"I've got a job to do," Phil said, folding his hands on the desk in front of him. "We've got four murders with no place to hang them. That makes me nervous, Tobias."

"I know. But I'm close. How about two more days?"

"No."

"One more. Twenty-four hours. We're talking about saving General MacArthur's reputation," I said. What I didn't say was that

I thought there was a chance I might have to save more than his reputation. I might have to save his life. I'd have to find Pintacki and find him fast.

"Twenty-four hours," Phil said. "And no more bodies."

"Twenty-four hours," I said, standing up. "And I'll be at your house for dinner on Sunday at three."

"If you're not in jail," Phil said.

"Right," I agreed and went out the door.

Seidman was sitting at his desk nearby. He looked up as I came out, saw no visible scars and nodded. I nodded back and headed toward the squad room door. The same cop was still smoking and thinking near the window. The two Oriental kids were still seated in front of Cawelti's desk and he still wasn't there. Another pair of cops, both in uniform, were standing in a corner and talking loudly about a pinup one of them had just stuck on the wall near the water fountain.

"Better than Grable," said one cop. "Look at them legs, that smile, those lips. Mary Marlin is Miss Blue Ribbon, for chrissake. The California Models' Guild ain't wrong."

"Not bad," agreed the other cop, "but not Grable either."

I stopped in front of Cawelti's desk.

"What'd you do?" I asked the girl.

"We did nothing," she said softly, to keep the boy on her shoulder from waking. "We were walking home from a friend's this morning."

"And you were arrested?"

"Yes," she said. "And my brother is frightened. He sleeps when he is frightened. My parents will be frightened."

"What did the cops say who picked you up?" I asked.

"That we were Japanese and should be in a camp," the girl said. "We are not Japanese. We are Chinese. They wouldn't believe us. My brother Chou was frightened. He didn't understand. He fought them, tried to help me and they hit us and brought us here. And the man who sits there." She pointed with her free hand at Cawelti's empty chair. "That man said we will go to jail."

I felt rather than heard someone at my side and I turned, expecting to see the red face of John Cawelti, but it was Seidman.

"You heard that?" I asked.

"I heard," he said. "I'll talk to Phil. They'll be okay."

The girl looked at both of us, trying to understand, and the dozing boy started to awaken. I smiled at her and she smiled back carefully. I went for the door.

12

I took a cab to No-Neck Arnie's and checked through my receipts for food and cabs to keep from thinking about Ann and Chinese girls with fear in their eyes.

"The sands in the hourglass are running out, Arnie," I said, when I got there and discovered that my Crosley hadn't arrived yet.

"I don't give a shit," grunted Arnie the short, stout and neckless, who probed for something in his teeth with greasy fingers. "I just cut my hand on a cylinder block. You thought over what I said about the gas-ration books?"

"I'm thinking," I said. "How about a loaner for the day?"

Arnie had paused in his work under the hood of a battered Dodge when I came in. Now he turned his small brown eyes back to his love, the mangled intestines of the machine.

"Don't have loaners," he said, shoving a wrench into a space between the engine and some wires. "Don't give loaners. My job's fixing cars. I don't fix teeth. I don't look for lost wives. I don't give no loaners."

"You are a lovely man, Arnie. Have any kids?" I asked.

"What's that got to do with tea in China?" he asked back.

"Nothing," I admitted. "You have anything running I can rent?"

"See the Chrysler in the corner?" he asked.

"Yeah," I said.

"Transmission's a little drunk but it goes. I'm working on it for a doctor. He's out of town. Maybe it's fine. Maybe it's not so fine. Twenty bucks and you can have it till four."

"Everything's twenty bucks with you," I said.

"Used to be everything was fifteen," he agreed. "But there's a war on."

"Twenty," I agreed.

"In advance," he said.

"I've only got nine in my pocket, and a Luger," I said.

"I'll take five, leave you four and you give me thirty-five when you pick up the Crosley," he said. "You can keep the Luger."

"Do I have a choice?"

"Who knows?" said Arnie. "All I know is you want the Chrysler, that's what you pay. Life's simple like that."

I gave him the five, promised the rest at four and got in the Chrysler before he could change his mind. I had the rest of the cash I'd gotten from Major Castle in my front pocket. I knew that I'd get more respect—and my Crosley back on time—if I didn't give Arnie cash in advance, and Castle's and MacArthur's money was running low.

I stopped at a diner on San Vincente, locked the Luger in the glove compartment, went inside and ordered a Pepsi and a grilled cheese with french fries. While the waitress was working on it, I called Castle's number again. The same voice answered and told me Major Castle wasn't available. I asked to speak to "the General." The voice at the other end hesitated and then came back with a firm: "There is no General here."

"Great," I said. "If a General shows up, tell him Toby Peters called. Tell him I've got some information he should have and that I'll do my best to get back to where I met him before."

"There is no General here," the voice repeated.

"Fine, but if you are surprised and amazed by the sudden appearance of a General, give him my message."

I hung up, headed for my grilled cheese, fries, and Pepsi and hoped for a miracle. As it turned out, I didn't have long to wait. When I went back to the doctor's Chrysler and opened the door, Pintacki stepped out of the doorway of a nearby used-furniture store and aimed a .45 at me.

A woman across the street looked toward us and then hurried away, minding her own business.

He didn't shoot. I didn't expect him to. He thought I had something he wanted and I knew he had something I wanted. He lowered the gun and stepped to the car door, motioning for me to get in behind the wheel. I got in and leaned over to let him in. He had the gun trained on me through the window. I could probably have hit the gas and pulled away before he could've got off a decent shot, but I didn't want to.

"I followed you," Pintacki explained as I drove forward, aware of the pistol in his lap aimed at my stomach. "I followed you from your ex-wife's house. I was waiting there for you in case Conrad and Wylie missed you and you came. I was inside when you knocked on the door and she tried, in spite of this gun at her neck, to help you get away, but I didn't want you to get away. I was going to push past her and stop you but that man came, the policeman. I should have shot you both but I controlled my impatience. I followed you to the police station. I heard on the police band of my car that Conrad and Wylie had been killed. What the police don't know is that you killed them to keep them from getting the MacArthur papers back."

He was talking quickly, with more than a touch of frenzy in his voice.

"What did you do to Ann?" I asked, trying to keep my voice low and soothing but knowing I was doing a bad job.

"I didn't have time to do what I should have done," he said. "I had to follow you. I locked her in a closet. I could have killed her the way you killed Conrad and Wylie."

"I didn't kill Conrad and Wylie," I said, but Pintacki wasn't listening.

"Doesn't matter. Doesn't matter. They're casualties," Pintacki said. "Casualties. This is a war, a revolution to save this country. God whispered in my ear. Not much of a whisper, mind you, but a whisper I could feel rather than hear. I need those papers to accomplish my ends. I need them. I had them right in my hand, this hand." He held up his fist to show me which hand we were talking about. "You know what the trouble with this world is?"

"Nazis and Japs," I said.

"Loose ends," Pintacki said, his hand clenching. "No discipline.

Not like the movies. Life can learn so much from the movies if life would only watch. Sometimes I think God gave us the movies like a secret message, a message waiting for us to read it and understand."

"I don't have the papers," I said.

"You're lying," said Pintacki. "I left them in the castle, in my desk."

"They weren't in your desk, but I know where they are," I said, pulling into Laurel Canyon and heading across the hills. "I'll make a deal with you. I'll tell you where they are and you tell me about the murders of Hower and Lansing."

Pintacki grimaced and reached over quickly to touch his shoulder. A spot of blood seeped through his shirt from the bullet wound he'd suffered on Mrs. Plaut's porch and had, apparently, bandaged without complete success. "I didn't kill them. Conrad and Wylie didn't kill them," he said. "We save our bullets for those who deserve them."

"Like me?" I asked.

"Just like you," he said with a maniacal grin as we ground up the hill toward Mulholland Drive.

There were no cars behind me. As we approached the top, I threw the Chrysler into neutral and let it drop backward with a jerk. Pintacki's neck snapped back, his wounded shoulder slamming against the door. He let out a scream and dropped the gun. I threw an elbow in his face and checked the rearview mirror. We were picking up speed and about to hit a curve. I stomped the brake hard and Pintacki shot forward, hitting his head on the windshield with a dull thud. A car came around the curve as the Chrysler stopped, and the driver almost shot over the edge into nowhere. He held on though, and took the turn on two wheels going past us. I put the Chrysler's parking brake on, grabbed Pintacki's pistol, threw it in the back seat, threw the Chrysler into first, released the brake and started up the hill again.

Pintacki seemed to be out cold, slumped on the floor in a not very neat bundle.

I had as much as I could probably get from him. It would have to be enough. When I dropped down the other side of the hill and eased around Ventura Boulevard in the San Fernando Valley, I left Pintacki and checked the trunk of the Chrysler. I found some insulated wire, used it to tie his hands and feet, dumped him in the back seat, and hoped he wouldn't bleed all over the doctor's upholstery.

I drove a few blocks farther to a hot dog stand and tried to reach Ann. There was no answer. I called the Wilshire Station and asked for Phil. He was out. Seidman was in. I asked him to get someone to Ann's apartment fast, that she was probably locked in a closet and that I'd explain later. He didn't ask any questions. I hung up and tried the number Major Oren Castle had given me. This time no one answered.

I got back in the car and headed toward Pasadena. Pintacki groaned once or twice in the back seat. I turned on the Chrysler's radio and picked up the second chorus of Helen Forrest singing "I've Heard That Song Before," with Harry James providing trumpet fills. I hummed along nervously to drown out Pintacki's groans.

"Bleeding to death," moaned Pintacki when I hit the outskirts of Pasadena and headed east on California Boulevard. I looked over the seat at him. The spot of blood was larger, but not much.

"You'll live," I said. "What's a little wound to a hero like you? If God wants you saved, he'll save you."

"It hurts like hell," he groaned. "Get me a doctor."

"You disappoint me," I said. "Would Victor McLaglen whine and whimper like this? Ronald Colman? Chester Morris? Hoot Gibson? This is life. Learn something from the movies."

"I'll get you, Peters," he whispered. "I'll get you. As the Lord is my witness."

"Pintacki," I said with a sigh, "you're giving me bad lines from B movies. Why don't you quiet down, work on your dialogue and come back when you've got something worth pitching."

I turned the radio louder. Helen and Harry were doing "He's My Guy." I thought about Ann in the closet and took a sharper than necessary right onto Fair Oaks Avenue into San Marino. Pintacki rolled against the front seat and said something forbidden in the movies. I made a left on Monterey Road and pulled in front of the gate to the estate where I'd met MacArthur. It didn't open. I got out of the car and walked to the gate. There was a little phone in a metal box. I opened the box and picked up the phone.

"Yes?" came a flat male voice.

"My name's Peters. I'm here to see the General."

"There's no Gen . . ."

"Tell him I have some answers for him," I said. "Tell him there may not be much time."

The phone went dead and I stood looking at the broad green leaves of the tropical trees that blocked a view of the house beyond the iron gates and fence. I jangled the change in my pocket, touched the Luger in my belt and wondered what Helen Forrest was singing now.

The gate clicked like a shotgun, cracked open for loading. I gave it a push and watched it swing inward with hardly a sound. Back in the car, I closed the door and looked over at Pintacki, whose eyes were closed. He was breathing evenly so I didn't worry. I drove through and started up the driveway. In the rearview mirror I watched the gate swing shut and through the open window I heard it close with a metallic shudder.

On the steps in front of the door to the house stood Major Oren Castle—bleak, trim, hair tight and short like a golf course lawn. He was in uniform, complete with tie and medals, and he stood at ease, hands behind his back.

"I've been calling you," I said.

"I've been unable to return your calls," he said. "The military situation has changed in New Guinea. The General will have to head back to Australia this afternoon."

"I need ten minutes of his time," I said, stepping up on the porch next to Castle and looking out at the broad lawn and trees swaying in a prestorm breeze.

Castle rocked on his heels twice and nodded his head. He turned, opened the door and stepped back so I could go inside. I didn't say anything about Pintacki in the back seat.

We walked silently through the house, me in the lead, Castle behind. We paused in front of the same door to the same room where I'd first met the General. Castle knocked and MacArthur called, "Come in."

Castle opened the door and in I went, with him behind. MacArthur was dressed in a neatly ironed pair of khaki trousers and a matching short-sleeve shirt. It was faintly military, but not quite. His hands were behind his back, his corncob pipe clenched between his teeth. The room was just as hot as it had been before.

"Major Castle, you may wait outside," MacArthur said.

"I'd like Major Castle to hear this," I said.

MacArthur bit his pipe stem a little harder. He wasn't used to people questioning his decisions and it was clear that he didn't like it. I could see that he was considering a less than polite answer, but he held it in and said, "Very well. Major Castle will remain. I see nothing in your possession which might be the missing money or the papers you were seeking."

"Right, General," I said, feeling that first trickle of sweat on my brow. I sat wearily, with Castle behind me and MacArthur in front. "I guess Major Castle briefed you on what happened in Angel Springs."

"He did," MacArthur said. "I know that Andrew Lansing is dead and that this man Pintacki killed him. I gather you have not found this man Pintacki and his henchmen."

"I found them," I said. "His two men are dead. Pintacki's in the back seat of the car in your driveway. He doesn't know where the papers are. He and his men came after me, thinking I had them. And, General, Pintacki and his men didn't kill anyone."

MacArthur was pacing and thinking, trying to get a step ahead of me, to take back center stage.

"The property just beyond this to the right, over there," he said, pointing out the window with his pipe. "That belongs to the Patton family, as does a good deal of the land around here. General Patton is a wealthy man, a fierce, headstrong man who may emerge as a political factor following this war. George Patton would be a mistake."

By this time, I knew that according to MacArthur anyone would be a mistake except Douglas MacArthur. I didn't say anything and he went on.

"Over there, to the left, just beyond that row of hedges, is the Huntington estate, library and gardens. Do you know what artifacts of Western civilization stand in the gallery and library over there?"

"Gainsborough's *Blue Boy*," I said. "And Lawrence's *Pinkie*. Did you know Pinkie was Elizabeth Barrett Browning's aunt? Her father's sister? Let's see. There's a Gutenberg Bible and . . ."

"That'll do," said MacArthur, less than pleased to be upstaged again.

I'd been to the Huntington at least twenty times when I was a kid. Glendale was just down the road. I even remember seeing old man Huntington himself back in 1910 or 1911 when I was in high school. He was a big guy with a white mustache walking alone down one of the garden paths he had built for the public. The teacher we were with, Miss Herbert, pointed him out to us. He didn't look like one of the richest men in the world. He looked like a sad old man with a lot on his mind. Old Man Huntington had put together the Pacific Electric Streetcar System, the big red cars and the yellow cars, the trackless trollies with the overhead electric cables that you could ride through the canyons for a dime. "The world's wonderland lines," he called it, and at its peak Huntington's Pacific Electric carried more passengers every day than the transit systems of the five biggest cities combined. MacArthur had picked the wrong hick to impress with California history.

"What do you have to tell me, Mr. Peters?" MacArthur said as he started to pace, hands behind his back. "And remember, brevity is essential. I have to leave at fifteen-thirty hours."

"I know who has the papers," I said.

"Excellent," he said.

"And I know who killed Hower, Lansing and Pintacki's men," I added.

"Fine," said MacArthur. "Will you now share this information with us? Who is it?"

"Major Castle," I said pointing a thumb over my shoulder in his direction.

13

"Major Castle?" MacArthur asked, stopping suddenly and looking at me as if I were more than a little insane.

I looked at Castle, who stood at ease and met my eyes. His were cold.

"The way I put it together," I said, "our Major Castle went to Hower's and Lansing's place for the papers. Lansing was gone. He persuaded Hower to tell him where Lansing had gone and then he killed Hower and left him for me and . . . an associate to find. He got to Angel Springs ahead of me and found Lansing, but Lansing had already turned the papers over to Pintacki. Our Major Castle shot Lansing and made a mistake."

"A mistake?" MacArthur said, looking at Castle.

"When Major Castle showed up in Angel Springs in record time and rode to our rescue," I continued, "he routed Pintacki and then helped me and my associate search for the papers. Pintacki told me today where he had hidden the papers. When we searched his place I'd looked there but they were gone."

"And that was Major Castle's mistake?" MacArthur said, humoring me.

"No," I said. "His mistake came when we drove past Lansing's body and Oren mentioned that Lansing had been shot in the back of the head. Lansing was on his back. There were no exit holes visible. He could have been shot in the back, stabbed, bludgeoned. You name it. I've got a witness, my associate, a trained Pinkerton agent."

I had MacArthur's interest now, if not his confidence. "Go on," he said and I did.

"Our Oren's next step was to see to it that Pintacki and his boys, when they were released, would be blamed for taking the papers. He couldn't have them going around looking for papers that they were supposed to have. But he didn't catch up with them in time. They came right for me. He didn't get to Conrad and Wylie till after they'd come to me for the papers. You following me so far, General?"

Distaste was evident on MacArthur's lips, but I didn't care whether he liked me so long as he believed me.

"I am," he said.

"I can go get Pintacki out of the car so you can hear it from him. He's not much fun but he's pretty convincing. All we have to do is bring him in, tell him we have the papers and you'll see that he believes it."

"Unconvincing," MacArthur said.

"But true," I insisted, wiping my sweating neck with my sleeve.

"Why would Major Castle kill four men to get my political papers?" asked MacArthur.

"Ask him," I suggested.

We both looked at Castle, who moved from his at-ease position to attention without being told. I could see a dark dot of perspiration just above his collar.

"Major," MacArthur said. "Do you have the papers we have been looking for?"

Castle's mouth quivered. The question was direct, an order from his commander. I'd have had five lies ready with variations as needed, but Castle was a career soldier. He hadn't counted on it coming to this.

"Yes, sir," Castle said, strain in his voice.

"Where are they?" MacArthur asked, hiding his surprise rather brilliantly.

"In my kit by the door ready for our debarkation," Castle said.

"Get them," MacArthur ordered.

Castle shuddered. He clenched his teeth and his eyes filled with tears.

"No, sir," he said.

"Major, I've issued an order," MacArthur said, stepping toward Castle.

"I'll have to disobey that order, sir," Castle said, tears now coming freely.

"Why on earth? . . ." MacArthur began. "You did kill those men?"

"I did, sir," said Castle.

"Explain, Major," MacArthur ordered.

"My friends . . . my . . ." Castle began, and then pulled himself together. "I watched them die around me on Bataan. For two and a half months I watched them die and you told us to hold the line. They died. Archie Stimson, that jug-eared Lieutenant. Do you remember him, General?"

"I do," said MacArthur, softly.

"Stimson died next to me," Castle said. "Wallford, Maas, hundreds of them and more died when the Japanese marched them across the island, and more are still dying, and why? Because you were too proud to back up. You sat in your cave on Corregidor and told us to die, and we did. You were a few miles away by boat and how many times did you come to Bataan, General?"

"I was in a vital command position," said MacArthur, softly.

"Once," Castle shouted. "Once in seventy-two days. You know what we called you?"

"Yes," said MacArthur, so softly that I could barely hear him.

"Dugout Doug," spat Castle.

"We were shelled on Corregidor, Major," MacArthur said. "We, my wife, my son, myself, were shelled and near starvation. We . . ."

"You can't be allowed to turn this country into another Bataan," said Castle. "Not if it means my life. No more Corregidors, General. I'm turning those papers over to someone who'll see to it that every radio station, every magazine, every major newspaper in this country sees them. You'll be lucky to keep your stars for a week. Pintacki wanted to use you. I know you can't be used. But you can be destroyed."

"Major," MacArthur said. "You won't destroy me. You'll

destroy the morale of this nation. You'll destroy it at a time when the United States needs to put its faith in General Douglas MacArthur."

"Sorry, General," Castle said. "You're just not that important. I could shoot you. I wouldn't hesitate for a second, but turning over those papers will destroy you every day of your arrogant life. I hope you live forever, General. I hope you live forever and suffer the way we did on Bataan."

"It's over, soldier," MacArthur said, gently. "Stand at ease and . . ."

"We sang a song on Bataan, General," Castle said, his voice cracking. "Would you like to hear it?"

"I think not, Major," MacArthur said, standing face to face with Castle.

"Dugout Doug MacArthur lies ashakin' on the Rock," Castle began singing it to the tune of "The Battle Hymn of the Republic," his voice cracking and slightly off-key:

> *Safe from all the bombers and from any sudden shock*
> *Dugout Doug is eating of the best food on Bataan*
> *And his troops go starving on . . .*
> *Dugout Doug come out from hiding*
> *Dugout Doug come out from hiding*
> *Send to Franklin the glad tidings*
> *That his troops go starving on.*

MacArthur's hand came up in a low arc. His open palm slapped against Castle's cheek, turning the Major's head to the right in a sudden jerk.

"Steady on, soldier," MacArthur whispered.

Castle's wet eyes blinked madly and fixed on MacArthur. I'd seen that kind of look before. Castle's hand went to the holster at his hip and came up with a pistol leveled at the General's stomach.

"Steady on, soldier," I said, showing the Luger I had eased into my lap.

MacArthur didn't blink, didn't flinch. He continued to meet Castle's eyes and I could see Castle glancing at my gun. Madness might overcome his plan, so I reminded him: "If you shoot the General, he won't suffer when you turn in the papers."

Major Castle took a deep breath, gulped and turned his army .45 in my direction.

It was a stand-off, though I had the uncomfortable feeling that if triggers were pulled I'd come out the worse for wear. I'd survived two other stand-offs in the last couple of days. I wasn't sure about this one. Castle knew how to use his gun. He was a pro and I was seated and in no hurry to start shooting in that small, hot room. I glanced at MacArthur. The son of a bitch still wasn't sweating.

Castle reached back for the doorknob, keeping his .45 aimed at me. MacArthur's right hand began to move and I said, "No, General."

MacArthur shot me a less-than-friendly look but dropped his hand as Castle backed out of the door and slammed it. I got out of the chair and MacArthur went to the phone.

When I stepped into the hall I saw Castle turning a corner. Behind me, MacArthur was barking orders into the phone. I followed the rapping of Castle's shoes ahead of me and peeked around the corner. He picked up a small khaki bag near the door, heard me behind him, turned and fired. The bullet cracked a mirror over my shoulder and I flattened myself against the wall. I heard the front door open and close and Castle's footsteps on the porch.

I took a breath, dried my palms against my pants, regripped the pistol and followed him out the door in a crouch. It took me a second to realize that he wasn't running down the driveway to the gate. He was on my right, running across the lawn, bag dangling from one hand, pistol in the other.

The first thunderclap from the coming storm crackled overhead like a massive short circuit. I went after Castle, fast as my back would let me. We went through a row of trees, and by the time he hit the rear fence I was losing ground. He threw the khaki bag over the fence, holstered the pistol and began to climb. It wasn't an easy feat, but he was lean, more than a little nuts and in good condition. He went over and came down on the other side with me about twenty yards away and panting, a fence between us.

He turned to me, put his hand to his holster, changed his mind and ran into the grounds of the Huntington estate. There was no gate that I could see. No break. I paused at the fence to catch my breath, put the Luger in my belt and started to climb. It took me about six or seven months to get to the top of the fence and a frightening moment of hell to make it over the pointed iron stakes at the top. By the time I hit ground on the other side, my legs were as wobbly as a middleweight who'd made it to the fifth round with Tony Zale.

Castle was nowhere in sight and I didn't know how well, if at all, he knew the Huntington grounds. It had been more than twenty years since I'd last been there, but if things hadn't changed too much I knew where I was.

I jogged across a flat lawn and past a pond filled with colorful carp who came toward me with curiosity and then backed away when they saw I didn't have anything. I didn't see any people, any visitors. Maybe the place was closed for additions or repairs. Maybe the threatening rain had driven them away. Thunder cracked again and the rain began to fall from the dark sky. I kept going past the main house. Nothing. I searched the grounds for about ten minutes and considered giving up but decided to turn left and head for the Oriental garden.

By the time I got to the entrance on the hill the rain was getting serious. I looked down at the swaying white flowers and the red drum bridge over the pond. Pellets of water popped in the pond and I had the feeling that I was in the right place. The hill facing the pond was empty. I walked down the path carefully and reached for the Luger in my belt. It wasn't there. I'd lost it along the way. I could have sworn until that very second that I felt it, chill and heavy, against my stomach. But all my swearing wouldn't make it so.

I was halfway down the path, blinking and wiping rain from my face, when Castle appeared on the red bridge. He had been crouched low behind the railing, apparently been watching me, and knew I had lost the gun.

"Stop," he called. He stood, the bag in his left hand, gun in his right aimed at me. The rain was in my favor. So was the distance. But he had had bad-weather shooting experience and there was nowhere to hide. A bush can't be relied upon to stop a bullet.

"I'm backing away, Major," I said, showing my hands.

"Too late, Peters," he said. "You'll have to die. It's not the way I want it, but I've got a mission and a lot of dead men counting on me."

"You've got it wrong, Oren," I said.

The shot tore a red rose from a stem at my left. No one could shoot that well. He'd either missed me or fired wide because, in spite of what he said, he still wasn't sure about what he wanted to do.

Another clap of thunder and a flash of lightning on the hill behind seemed to help him make up his mind. He leveled the .45 in my direction and I closed my eyes.

The shot came, sharp and close and from the wrong direction. I opened my eyes and saw Castle glaring past me up the hill. I turned and watched Douglas MacArthur, my Luger in his right hand, gun leveled at Castle, walking down the path. MacArthur's eyes didn't blink, and even though he was soaked through he looked fresh and confident.

"It's over, Major," MacArthur called. "I don't wish to shoot you."

Castle laughed and stared up into the rain which pelted his face and mouth.

"It's not over, General," he said, holding up the khaki bag.

MacArthur's arm went level and he sighted along it. He was a few feet behind me, and when he pulled the trigger it was followed by a recoil of lightning over the San Gabriel Mountains. On the drum bridge, Major Castle tottered and dropped the bag. It fell into the pond and began to sink. Blood mixed with rain and trailed down his left arm.

Castle screamed at the sky and let out a pained cry I could only imagine in my worst nightmares.

"Come down, Major," MacArthur called, stepping past me.

"Gone," cried Castle. "It's gone. Now all I can do is kill you. It's not enough. It's not fair and it's not enough, but it's all I've got."

The .45 came up again and leveled at the advancing MacArthur, who didn't pause. MacArthur had lost the advantage. He could have shot Castle a second time while he ranted, but he let the opportunity pass, dropped the Luger and continued down the path.

"Major," MacArthur commanded. "You have a direct order to put that weapon away and come down here."

"General," I shouted, going down the steps for the Luger. Castle turned and fired. I stopped and went rigid.

"I hope you burn forever in hell," Castle said, turning the gun back on MacArthur.

"That is between me and my God," MacArthur said. "If I am to be punished, it will be by my maker and not by you or any other man."

And MacArthur kept walking along the path and to the bottom of the bridge, no more than twenty feet from Castle, who stood above him clutching the red wooden bridge railing with his wet bloody hand.

MacArthur's eyes never left the face of the man on the bridge as he began to climb the steps. I stood watching, knowing that the best I could do was go for the Luger and get off a shot or two after he shot the General. If I was lucky, I'd hit him and maybe MacArthur would survive. I wasn't feeling lucky.

MacArthur climbed the stairs, swiftly reducing the chances for his survival and mine. I bent, deciding on a dive and roll that would put me in the hospital if I were lucky enough to survive.

When he was no more than three feet from Castle at the top of the half-moon bridge, MacArthur held out his hand for the gun and Castle handed it to him.

"Oh, God," cried Castle, going to his knees.

MacArthur stepped forward and took the man's head against his chest.

I was too far away and the rain was too loud and heavy to be sure of everything MacArthur said next, but I'm sure that the first four softly spoken words were, "It's all right, son."

14

When we got back to the house MacArthur turned Castle over to two armed soldiers, whom he ordered to treat the Major with "the respect his military record merited." The rain had slowed to a trickle and I was tired, tired and heavy. I had a mental flash of Jeremy's damned hourglass and I felt depressed.

"I've seen this too many times and in too many wars," MacArthur said as Castle was ushered away in a military car. "Good men. Good soldiers. Major Castle is a good soldier."

"Not for me to judge, General," I said. "I'll have to report this to my brother. He's a captain in the L.A.P.D. Have someone call him and work it out. His name's Pevsner, Phil Pevsner in the Wilshire Station. He was a good soldier in the last war. Rainbow Division. One of your boys. Wounded."

"Give him my best and my thanks," the General said, holding out his hand. I took it.

"I appreciate your professional assistance," he said. "A check will be forwarded to you from a personal account. The name on it will be McBridge. I cannot be in the position of having to explain why I am writing checks to a private investigator."

"I understand, General," I said.

He looked at his watch and smiled sadly.

"I have a plane to catch and I must shower and change," he said.

Those were his last words to me as he turned the corner past the mirror which had been shattered by Castle's shot. I left the house and got in the Chrysler.

"What is happening?" Pintacki demanded as I turned in the driveway. "What was all that shooting? Whose place is this?"

I didn't talk. I drove in the puddled streets and tried to find Helen Forrest again. I was wet, tired and miserable. Where was Helen Forrest when I needed her most? I couldn't find her or Harry James or Ziggy Elman or Tex Beneke. I turned off the radio and told Pintacki if he didn't shut up I'd lock him in the trunk. I meant it. He knew it and shut up.

I delivered Pintacki to the Wilshire Station and turned him over to Phil, who had already received a call from one of MacArthur's aides. They were working out what to do about Castle. We didn't say much. I told Phil that MacArthur had given him his best and Phil looked touched.

"Ann's fine," he said as a uniformed cop led Pintacki away, squalling for his attorney. "He didn't hurt her. Just shoved her in the closet."

"I'll get right over there," I said, and turned to leave.

"She doesn't want to see you, Toby," Phil said. "She said you'd brought the old life back again and she didn't want it. Go home, take a shower and get in bed. You look awful. And give Ann some time."

"I'll do what I have to do, Phil," I said.

"You'll stay away from Ann or I'll bend you, Toby," he said evenly. "Believe me."

"Okay, I believe you," I said. "I'll give it a while. I'll see you, Ruth and the kids on Sunday."

"You do that," he said, turning back into the squad room and not looking back.

I got the Chrysler back to No-Neck Arnie's just after four. He charged me an extra five. I paid it and listened to him talk about gas-ration books for a minute or two before I cut him off and told him I was soaked and tired. He let me go with a "just think about the books. All I ask."

Shelly was gone when I got to the office just before five. The place looked as if a cleaning woman had died halfway through her monthly work. Shelly hadn't done any more on the office since I'd left. I half expected an angry note. There *was* a scrawled note taped to my office door, but it wasn't angry. It said that Shelly had hired Louise-Marie as his receptionist-assistant and that I was to call a Mr. Hammett. Shelly went on to say that Hammett had explained that he had to leave town on an emergency and would be sending Shelly a check for inconveniencing him. The last words on the note were: "You are forgiven."

I sloshed into my office, sniffled a few times, blew my nose and threw the handkerchief in the trash can under my desk. Then I called Hammett. He was, he said, about to check out of the hotel.

"A friend of mine recommended a dentist in Albany, New York," he said. "Should be quiet there."

"Good luck," I said.

"Is it over?" he asked.

"Over," I said.

"Castle?" he asked.

"Castle," I said. "He bumped Wylie and Conrad, too. Cops have Pintacki. I don't know who gets Castle, the military or the L.A. District Attorney. The army has him now. Thanks again for the help."

"My pleasure," said Hammett. "Proved I can still handle myself. Now all I have to do is prove it to the army."

"Good luck," I said with a sneeze.

"I'll look you up when the war's over, Toby," he said and hung up.

I went to Jeremy's office but it was dark and locked. I'd hoped to run into Alice and congratulate her on the baby, but it was probably just as well I didn't come near her. I seemed to be coming down with something from my romp in the rain through the Huntington estate.

I drove back to Mrs. Plaut's, hungry, wet and coming down with a cold.

She caught me five steps up.

"Mr. Peelers," she said triumphantly. "You missed the tumult and uproar this morning. I rousted an invasion of Nazis who were looking for you."

"Congratulations," I said.

"You are welcome," she said. "You look a fright. Where is my man-u-scrip?"

"The Nazis got it," I said.

Mrs. Plaut looked startled.

"Why on earth would they want a chapter of my family chronicles?"

"I don't know," I said. "It is sometimes difficult to fathom the devious mind of a Nazi."

"Don't I know it," she said. "Fortunately, I made a carbon copy and will deliver it to your room presently. In the meanwhile, take a hot bath and I will mix you a toddy."

"Thank you," I said. I pulled myself up the stairs and slogged to my room where I peeled off my clothes, wrapped a slightly used towel around my waist and headed for the bathroom. I got in the tub with my nub of Lifebuoy soap, turned on the tap and sat while the hot water trickled slowly against my toes.

Mrs. Plaut appeared about five minutes later, with the water no more than three inches high. She burst through the door and placed a steaming drink on the bathroom stool which she had kicked next to the tub.

"I'm in the tub, Mrs. Plaut," I said.

"I am not blind," she said, crossing her arms. "Drink. It will make you feel better. My mother's concoction."

"I am naked," I said over the trickling water.

"We are born naked, Mr. Peelers," she said. "And you are not such a vision as to drive me to passion. Only the late mister could do that, Lord rest his bones."

She left only when I had sipped the toddy, pronounced it good, which it was, and promised to finish it all. The toddy was definitely alcoholic.

I got out of the tub about half an hour later, dried myself, returned the soap to the communal medicine cabinet, brushed my teeth with Teel and returned to my room. I found Gunther Wherthman sitting on my sofa, his feet a good six inches from the floor and the cat in his lap. Gunther, as always, was dressed in an immaculate three-piece suit. This one was dark brown.

"Toby," he said in his Swiss accent. "I am pleased to see you well. I hope you do not mind my coming into your room."

"Not at all, Gunther," I said, sinking down on my mattress on the floor. "I spent the night in your room. Don't ask me. I'll explain it after I've had some sleep. How was your trip to San Francisco?"

"Excellent," he said, petting the cat, whose eyes closed contentedly. "I translated three librettos from French and one from German for possible English language presentation for the opera."

"Terrific," I said. "How about dinner after I get a few hours' sleep?"

"By all means," Gunther said. "I stopped for provisions and will prepare something light."

"Something heavy will be fine, Gunther," I said. "Something very heavy."

"As you wish, Toby," he said. "But my call is a bit more than social."

I looked at Gunther blearily.

"You've got a problem?"

"Not I," he said. "An acquaintance I worked with in San Francisco. It is rather delicate, and I suggested that I knew someone who might be of some assistance to him."

"San Francisco," I said. "Who's the client?"

"Leopold Stokowski," he said.

"I'll give him a call tomorrow," I said.

"The cat? He is yours?" Gunther asked.

"Let's share him, Gunther," I said. "If it's all right with you."

"That will be acceptable," Gunther said, placing the cat gently on the sofa and climbing down. "What is his name?"

"Dash," I said.

"A rare name," said Gunther, walking to the door. "What is its origin?"

"A guy who gave me a hand," I said, closing my eyes and putting my head back on the pillow.